Wild Thing

✶✶✶✶✶

Winnie

The Horse Gentler

1

Tyndale House Publishers, Inc.
Carol Stream, Illinois

Wild Thing

DANDI DALEY MACKALL

Visit Tyndale's exciting Web site for kids at www.tyndale.com/kids and the
Winnie the Horse Gentler Web site at www.winniethehorsegentler.com.

You can contact Dandi Daley Mackall through her Web site at
www.dandibooks.com.

Tyndale Kids logo is a trademark of Tyndale House Publishers, Inc.

Wild Thing

Copyright © 2002 by Dandi Daley Mackall. All rights reserved.

Cover photograph copyright © 2001 by Bob Langrish. All rights reserved.

Interior horse chart given by permission, Arabian Horse Registry
of America®. www.theregistry.org

Designed by Jacqueline L. Nuñez

Edited by Ramona Cramer Tucker

Scripture quotations are taken from the *Holy Bible*, New Living Translation,
copyright © 1996. Used by permission of Tyndale House Publishers, Inc.,
Carol Stream, Illinois 60188. All rights reserved.

This novel is a work of fiction. Names, characters, places, and incidents
either are the product of the author's imagination or are used fictitiously.
Any resemblance to actual events, locales, organizations, or persons, living
or dead, is entirely coincidental and beyond the intent of either the author
or publisher.

For manufacturing information regarding this product, please call
1-800-323-9400.

ISBN 978-0-8423-5542-1, mass paper

Printed in the United States of America

15 14 13 12 11 10 09
18 17 16 15 14 13 12

For Jen,
my daughter,
my friend,
my fellow writer,
my fellow rider

My mom used to say, "Winnie Willis, in the beginning God created heaven and earth and horses. And sometimes I have to wonder if the good Lord shouldn't have quit while he was ahead."

She knew that was how I felt. She always knew.

I wished Mom could have been right here with me, riding bareback, riding double. Instead, white fog thick as a horse's tail made everything feel upside down as my sister and I headed home from the stable, keeping to the dirt path. I'd never thought of July in Ohio as foggy.

Lizzy, my "little sis," darted past me to walk the dirt path backwards while talking as fast as a horse's trot. At 11 years old—a solid year younger than me—she towers two inches over me. We both got Mom's green eyes and dark hair, but Lizzy dodged the freckles. Lizzy claims my voice is low and raspy and would sound great on the radio, but I think I always sound a little hoarse.

"Winnie?" Lizzy's voice, usually soft as a Morgan mare's winter coat, sharpened. "Have you heard a word I've said?"

"Nope," I answered, picking up the scent of pines and poplar trees from the fields . . .

. . . *and maybe horse?*

At least a half mile behind us was Stable-Mart, the sorry excuse for a stable, where I had the royal job of mucking out stalls. Anything to be near horses.

"I said . . . ," Lizzy shouted, like the problem was something her volume could fix, "I'm cooking my famous tuna casserole—Dad's favorite. I want him to *love* living in Ashland!"

I sighed.

"Winnie!" Lizzy said. "Dad could yank us out of Ohio and move us again to who-knows-where!"

I shrugged.

"How can you not care? I want to go to the

whole sixth grade here!" Lizzy demanded. "I can't even remember where I finished fourth grade! Today Eddy Barker asked me where I'd gone to fifth grade. I told him, 'The *I* states—Illinois, Indiana, and . . .' What was the last one? Oh yeah—'Iowa.' Well not this year! Huh-uh! No way, Winnie."

I could remember every school, down to the missing *L* in Mil_er Elementary. I could picture the cracks in my desk in Chicago, the paint at the left bottom corner of the window in Des Moines Middle School.

When I was in first grade in Wyoming, we found out I have a photographic memory. *Not* a super memory—just a photographic one. If my mind doesn't snap a picture when something happens, I still forget stuff.

Dad always thought I should be a better student, back when he thought about things like that. I admit, sometimes my memory works great on names and dates for history tests. It's like I can still see words and numbers on a page.

But a photographic memory is not so great for getting rid of pictures I *don't* want in my head—like the upside-down car and my mother's arm, limp as a ribbon over the steering wheel.

I picked up a rock and pitched it as far as I could. We'd moved five times in the two years since we'd sold our ranch in Wyoming. Ashland, Ohio, didn't seem much different than the other places, only smaller.

"Well, *you* may not care about anything, Winnie," Lizzy continued, "but I do! I like it here. Crickets! Ponds filled with frogs! Roly-polies—the cutest little bugs! And I've never seen so many trees—"

"Lizzy, shush!" I held out my hand like I was stopping traffic. The ground shook—not much, but enough.

Fog pressed against my eyeballs.

Ahead of us, from down the hill through the mist, something thumped.

"Don't tell me to—!" Lizzy started.

"Shh-hh!" I strained to hear it—*ta-dump, ta-dump, da-dump, da-dump,* closer and louder.

Horses!

"Move!" I shouted, shoving Lizzy toward the ditch.

DA-DUMP! DA-DUMP! Louder and louder.

"Four of them—no, five!" I yelled, as Lizzy stumbled into the ditch, sputtering something I couldn't make out. I held my ground, knowing

4

they couldn't be more than a few horses' lengths away.

One of the horses whinnied, a frightened burst of horse sadness and fear that tore at my heart.

"Winnie!" Lizzy screamed from the ditch. "Get out of the way!"

The sound of the horses' hooves pounded inside my chest. I made out a blur of legs under the fog cloud—hooves, pasterns, cannons. The stride of the lead horse made her about 15 hands high.

Like a vision, a white mare, silky mane flying, burst through the fog in front of me.

"Easy, girl," I said, raising my arms shoulder high, making a *T* with my body. "What's the rush?" I held my scarecrow position, not moving, as four other horses closed in behind the mare.

The fog-white horse skidded in front of me, back legs crouching. She reared, pawing the fog, as if fighting invisible cloud horses. Two smaller horses parted behind her, snorting, not knowing whether to head for the hills or wait for her to do battle for all of them.

But I couldn't take my eyes off the ghostly

mare. In the fog she appeared pure white. Her dish jowls, big eyes, and finely carved head left no doubt that she was Arabian. Arabians have black skin, but hers barely showed through her cloud-white coat, only casting a gray shadow near her leg joints.

"You the boss here?" I asked.

Two Quarter Horses, a bay Thoroughbred, and a sunburned black Standardbred formed a half-circle audience.

The mare continued to rear, her front hooves striking the ground, then springing up again. But her heart wasn't in it. The springs grew shorter until they stopped. From the scars at her hocks, her jagged hooves, tangled mane, and the wrinkles above her eyes, no one had loved her for a long time, if ever.

I held the mare's attention in a kind of horse bluff as I muttered to her and kept my position. If I gave in first, she'd figure she ruled me too. And I'd better dive out of her way fast. But if I could make her give to me, she'd know she didn't need to protect herself or her herd from me.

From the ditch, Lizzy started, "Winifred Will—!" But she stopped. Lizzy doesn't like horses, but she knows enough not to yell around them.

She'd seen our mother talk down dozens of hot horses.

Finally, the ghost mare blinked. She looked down, licking her lips, telling me, *Okay, I'll let you handle this.*

"That's my girl," I said, stepping closer. I touched her withers, the high part of her back between the shoulder blades. She let me scratch her neck under her tangled, white mane.

I felt horses galloping a second before I heard the thunder of more hooves. But these sounded different, closer to the ground. The fog had lifted a bit, and I squinted to see two men on chestnut Quarter Horses cantering up the path toward us.

"There they are!" one of the men cried. I knew by his snakeskin boots that he was the Spidells' son, Richard. Richard liked to play stable boss at his dad's Stable-Mart. He reminded me of an overgrown kid playing cowboy. The Spidells owned just about everything in Ashland and never let anybody forget it.

Richard sped up, galloping straight for us. "You! Kid! Get out of the way!"

The Arabian laid back her ears. I felt fear creep back into her muscles as Richard's gelding pulled up beside us.

"Grab that wild animal!" the older man yelled, riding up beside Richard.

The man's voice startled the mare. She whinnied, then reared once and bolted.

"Help!" Lizzy cried, as the mare headed straight for the ditch—Lizzy's ditch.

"Lizzy, get down!" I yelled.

The mare never broke stride. She galloped to the ditch and sailed over it, clearing with two feet to spare, her white tail high as a flag.

"Great!" Richard muttered.

The other horses stirred, but looked as if they'd had enough fun for one day and were ready to be led and fed.

"I'll take these on to the stable. You go after Wild Thing!" Richard shouted at the man, keeping the easy job for himself.

The man's belly bounced over his saddle horn. His stirrups hung too short, so his legs doubled. He cursed, then took his anger out on his mount, kicking his heels into the docile Quarter Horse.

"You are *so* human," I muttered.

The poor horse grunted and sprang like a Lipizzaner, then charged the ditch. But instead of taking it, he did a cattle-pony stop that nearly unseated his rider.

"What's the matter with you?" the man shouted, scrambling to get his seat back. Jerking the reins and regaining his stirrups, he let his horse take the long way down the path.

"Who was that?" I asked, staring after the vanishing white mare.

"That?" Richard said, circling his horse behind the abandoned herd. "Craig Barnum. He does the horse auctions. He's worthless—couldn't even get this lot from the auction barn to our stable."

"Not him," I said, squinting for the faintest view of the gorgeous mare. "The Arabian. Who is she?"

"She's a wild thing," Richard said, spitting the words out. "Dad bought her at auction. He got stung though, if you ask me. That mare's nothing but trouble."

Lizzy crawled out of the ditch as Richard trotted off, rounding up the other auction horses.

"Winnie?" Lizzy called. "Coast clear?"

I kept staring at the spot on the horizon where I'd last seen the beautiful, white ghost horse. My photographic memory had snapped a shot, leaving the horse's image seared into my brain.

"Winnie!" Lizzy shouted, coming to stand next to me. "What are you looking at?"

"The horse I've been dreaming about my whole life."

It was the truth, even though I'd hardly made the connection before the words came out of my mouth. For as long as I could remember, when I'd closed my eyes, I'd been able to picture an Arabian—noble, white, wide-eyed— exactly like this one.

"What are you talking about?" Lizzy demanded.

"Lizzy," I said, calling up my mind's picture of the rearing Arabian, "I have to have that horse. And I'll do whatever it takes to get her."

ea!" Lizzy squealed. "Now *that* sounds like the old Winnie!"

I turned to look at my sister for the first time since I'd shoved her into the ditch. Mud-caked hair hung over her face.

"Lizzy, are you all right?" I brushed off her khaki shorts, expecting her to be mad at me.

Instead she grinned as she stared into her clasped hands.

"This is so cool, Winnie!" Lizzy exclaimed. "A king-size God thing!"

A king-size God thing. Mom used to say that for everything from finding a robin's egg to the smell of a horse or the sound of a train in the distance. When Mom said it, Dad would raise his eyebrows and grin at her or maybe squeeze her shoulder.

I tried to examine Lizzy's skinned elbow, but she jerked it away.

"Careful! Wait 'til you see what I found! Right there in the ditch where you shoved me and the horse almost jumped in on top of me and trampled me to death."

"Sorry," I said.

"No! I never ever would have found it if you hadn't pushed me face-first into that ditch!" she exclaimed. "I mean, there I was, mud squishing into my nose, dried ditch grass poking my eyes, herds of wild horses waiting to knock my block off if I so much as raised my chin!" Lizzy took a deep breath. "And that's when I spied a patch of blue."

"A patch of blue? Facedown in the ditch?" I asked, wondering if she'd hit her head.

"Yes!" Lizzy twirled, keeping her clasped hands in front of her. "A gorgeous, incredible, heavenly blue—which could only mean one thing!"

I had no idea what she was talking about.

"The blue belly! Winnie, I found a blue-bellied fence lizard! What are the chances of that? I mean, how many spiny lizards are there in Ohio?"

"Seven?" I guessed.

"Winnie, I'm serious!" Lizzy insisted. "Okay, so it's no skink or gecko. But we're not in the desert or the tropics. So what do you expect, right? Fence lizards are tree climbers!"

I peered between Lizzy's thumbs to see her prize. The lizard was chubbier than I expected, with a tail as long as its body, three or four inches. I couldn't see the blue but had no real desire to.

"What are you going to do with it?" I asked, taking a step backward.

"Him," she corrected.

I didn't ask how she'd come by that information. "Okay. Him."

"I'll call him Larry," Lizzy said dramatically. "And I'll love him forever. And I'll make a home for him." She locked me in her stare. "So we *have* to stay here, Winnie! We just have to!" Lizzy glanced in the direction of the disappearing horses. "Only . . . are you sure about that horse? We could find you a nicer horse instead of that wild one."

I could still smell the Arabian's heat. "She's not wild, Lizzy," I said. "She just needs me to love her."

•

We walked without talking—at least not to each other. Lizzy kept up a steady stream of chatter with Larry the blue-bellied lizard.

And I tried to talk to God.

I know we haven't had much to say to each other lately, I prayed. *Since Mom's . . . well, you know . . . it's tough to talk to you. So I'm sorry to be coming just because I want something. But I guess you already know—I want that Arabian. I want to love her. I want her more than anything in my whole life . . . except for wanting Mom back.*

We turned onto our street, taking the broken sidewalk until it ran out. That's where our rental house sits. Dad chose it because it was the last house in town, for real.

Our yard is a work-in-progress. That's what Dad calls all the junk littering the grass, waiting for him to fix. He can fix anything if people will give him enough time and if he doesn't get sidetracked by one of his inventions. People would never believe he used to wear a suit and tie and order people around 12 hours a day in a fancy insurance office.

Under a big oak tree, as if dropped from its branches, were spokes and gears and bike tires—all part of Dad's latest invention—the backward bike. Behind the house sits an old barn in the middle of an overgrown pasture. Anybody passing by would think this is a junkyard.

Lizzy stepped through the opening in the low metal fence and stumbled over a spool of wire. She caught herself and widened her green eyes at me. "So you'll talk to Dad? Tell him we refuse to move!"

"Me?" I protested. "Why me?"

"Because I've been saying it for two years, Winnie!" Lizzy shouted. "He'll listen to you."

I shook my head. "I'm the last person Dad would listen to, Lizzy. You ought to know that by now." Since the accident, Dad had barely looked at me, much less listened to me. I didn't blame him. It's just the way things were now.

"Winifred Winnie Willis!" Lizzy exclaimed, pulling out all the stops. "You said you would do whatever it takes to make that wild horse yours!"

"Yeah," I admitted. "But I was thinking more along the lines of jumping out of a moving car or walking through fire or wrestling a barrelful of bears—something a little easier than talking to Dad."

I hadn't asked Dad for anything since the accident. When he sold the ranch, I didn't ask to keep a single horse. When he sold off Mom's saddles, I didn't ask him to please save just one, just in case. Each time he'd announce we were moving again, I never whined like Lizzy did. I never even asked where we were moving.

Lizzy held her head so close to mine I could see myself in her eyes. "Well?"

I bit my lip and touched the tiny horseshoe scar just below my elbow—a reminder of the accident, as if I needed one.

"I'll do it," I said. "I'll talk to Dad."

"Sweet!" Lizzy did a skyrocket cheerleader cheer. But she came down on a sheet of metal Dad was using to repair somebody's lawn mower. Losing her balance, she tilted backward. I grasped her wrist to keep her from falling. Her hands flew apart. The lizard slipped out into the yard, where it found a zillion places to hide.

"Larry!" Lizzy cried, dropping to her hands and knees.

I saw the lizard wiggle under a bike pump. "There he is!"

We bumped into each other reaching for him. Larry scooted under a pile of kindling, and the chase was on.

"Larry, come here!" Lizzy screamed.

We zigzagged across the yard, around the house, losing him, then spying him wriggling through the grass.

Then he was gone.

We turned over logs, looked inside an old milk can, shook bushes.

"Lizzy," I said, sweat dripping from my forehead, "you'll find another one. You can call him Larry II."

Lizzy shot me a warning glare. Mom used to say Lizzy was her little Trakehner. Trakehner horses were ridden by knights because they'd go anywhere, do anything, and never say die. Lizzy would never say die until we found Larry.

"Come on," I said. "Maybe he slithered his way into that old barn."

In the three weeks we'd been in Ohio and called the rental house home, we'd never ventured into the faded brown-red barn. I shoved back the wooden door and stepped inside. Sunlight streaked the floor, beaming in through spaces between slats. Dust danced in the lasers like tiny bubbles in a waterfall.

We stood side by side, taking it all in. Against the far wall, hay bales were stacked to the ceiling. Stalls faced each other across a wide stallway,

a middle aisle that ran the length of the barn.
Through the dirt and dust I smelled old manure.
I could almost see my white Arabian prancing
around this barn. This is where I'd keep her.

"Larry?" Lizzy called timidly.

Something darted between bales.

Scritch . . . scritch scratch . . . scritch!

"Wh-what was that?" I asked.

Lizzy didn't answer. We listened to more
scurrying coming from some unseen world I'd
just as soon not see.

"Lizzy," I whispered, "do you think it's rats?"

"Cats," came the answer behind us, a male
voice.

I swung around, my heart thumping. Lizzy
had fists raised for battle.

We were facing a tall, thin kid who might not
have been much older than me. He looked like
people in old movies from the 60s or 70s, with
long, wavy blond hair; gold, wire-rimmed glasses;
blue-striped, flared jeans; and an orange-and-pink,
tie-dyed shirt like we'd made in grade school.

"Cats," he repeated quietly. "Not rats."

I hadn't even heard him creep in. "This is
private property," I warned, not smiling.

"Winnie!" Lizzy scolded. She whisked her hair

back and twisted it into a ponytail that looked better than my hair does after 15 minutes of struggling with it. She stuck out her hand and shook his. "I'm Lizzy Willis."

He nodded. "Catman, Catman Coolidge."

I didn't offer my name.

"This your twin?" he asked, tilting his head my way.

Lizzy giggled as if we hadn't been asked that a thousand times. At least he hadn't asked if I was the little sis, like some people do.

"This is Winnie," Lizzy explained. "I'm 11 and she's12." She narrowed her eyes as she sized him up. "Bet you're . . . 14? No . . . 13!"

"Right-on," he answered.

"We're looking for Larry, my lizard," Lizzy continued. "Have you seen him? He's seven inches long, with a blue band around his throat and blue on either side of his belly, and—"

"Looks like a snake with legs," I said.

"Winnie!" Lizzy exclaimed. "Don't mind my rude sister. Mother used to say Winnie is a Mustang. Those feisty horses that like to live by themselves in the mountains?"

No wonder people think Lizzy is the older

sister. She's a hundred times more in control and at ease with people than I am.

Lizzy surveyed the barn. "You know, I'll bet Larry's found himself a good spot in here. I didn't want him to be caged anyway."

"Far out," Catman said. "Cats won't bother him."

Half a dozen heads poked out from between the bales—cats—gray, black, orange. I took a step toward them, and they darted like the hay was on fire.

"We can't have wild cats in here," I said, imagining how they might spook the Arabian.

"Not wild," Catman said, walking right up to the mountain of hay. He stuck his hands in his pockets, threw back his head, and let out an eerie screech: *"Keeeeee-y!"*

All at once he was swarmed by more cats and kittens than I'd ever seen on the face of the earth. They pressed around him like he was the Pied Piper of Ashland, Ohio. A reddish, longhaired cat as big as a cocker spaniel rubbed at his bell-bottoms, while a litter of spotted kittens sharpened their claws on his ankles.

Lizzy leaned over and whispered, "Winnie, Catman rocks!"

"See?" he said, reaching down and petting a dozen cats who couldn't get close enough to him. "Not wild—feral. Part wild."

"Look," I said firmly. My voice sent the cats racing back to the bales. "They can't stay. I'm . . . we're going to have horses in here. It's a horse barn."

Behind his small, round glasses, Catman's eyes looked Siamese blue. "Cats were here first."

"But it's *our* barn!" I insisted.

"Don't think so," he said calmly.

My face felt like fire. "Yeah? Well, we'll just see about that, *Catman!* We'll see who pays the rent. Horses are in—cats are out!"

"Winnie!" Lizzy had moved to the barn door. "Dad's home!"

I shot Catman one last frown, which he returned with a catlike grin. Then I stormed out of the barn.

Dad either didn't hear us calling, or he pretended he didn't. He strode straight into the house without so much as a glance our way, leaving the motor of the old cattle truck running. The truck was the only vehicle Dad had kept, and he was probably the only one who could keep it running.

By the time Lizzy and I reached the house, Dad came flying out, a suitcase in each hand, his sunglasses on top of his head.

"Don't just stand there gawking," Dad said, stepping around me to the truck and flinging suitcases inside. "Get your things. We're moving."

$\mathcal{D}$ad, no!" Lizzy squealed, bursting into tears.

Dad stopped, wiped his forehead, and put a hand on Lizzy's shoulder. His tan work coveralls made him look like an astronaut. I wouldn't have been surprised if he'd told us we were off to the moon.

"I'm thinking this town is too small for an odd-job man," Dad said, his voice flat. "But Pittsburgh—"

My stomach knotted until I thought I'd hurl.

What am I thinking? I don't deserve a normal life. Or a horse like that! Not after what I did. If it weren't for me, we'd still be in Wyoming with Mom. I know it, and Dad knows it. And neither one of us will ever forget it.

Anger surged through my chest, down my

leg, and came out in a field-goal kick to the nearest object—one of Dad's bike tires. My toe throbbed as I watched the tire fly up, then crash at the feet of the Catman.

Lizzy and Dad stopped arguing, stunned to silence. Catman picked up the tire and examined the spokes.

I wasn't mad at Dad or anybody else. I was mad at me. But there stood Catman, who had snuck up on us like a cat burglar.

"What do *you* want?" I snapped. "You win. Your stupid cats can live happily ever after in that run-down barn. No horses. No Willis family. Congratulations!"

Catman stared at the spokes as if I weren't shouting at him. "Do this yourself?" he asked, glancing at Dad. His long fingers cupped the gears.

Dad left Lizzy and joined Catman. Side by side, they made an odd pair. Dad, with dark, curly hair and a deep tan from working outside instead of at the insurance office like he used to, looked like a negative of Catman's pale skin and blond hair.

"It's something I'm experimenting with," Dad said, flipping a metal lever on the gear.

Catman spun the tire. "You reversed the whole thing."

Dad looked surprised. "I did."

"Did it work?" Catman asked. "When you crossed the chain and reassembled, did it go backward?"

"Yes!" The edge came back to Dad's voice the way it did when he talked about his inventions. "It took 14 tries, but I got it working."

Catman followed Dad to the tin lean-to beside our house. Lizzy and I trailed along, exchanging raised-eyebrow looks.

"First, second, third, right?" Catman said, pointing out each of the bikes in the shed.

"Right!" Dad said. "I learned more each time."

Catman dropped to his back for a better look. "Cool."

"You like it?" Dad asked, obviously pleased to find somebody who appreciated his genius. Dad's inventions usually ended up embarrassing Lizzy and me.

"Winnie," Dad said, not looking at me, "demonstrate the *back bike* for . . . I'm sorry. What was your name?"

"Catman Coolidge," he said.

Dad unlocked the bike. "Winnie, take a spin around the yard for Mr. Coolidge."

"Dad—," I started.

"Do it, Winnie!" Lizzy whispered.

I sighed but got on.

"Don't forget!" Dad shouted as I pushed off and pedaled backward. "Brake to the front!"

The bike doesn't really go backward. It goes frontward. Otherwise it would be dangerous. The backward part comes in pedaling.

I pedaled backward, and the bike eased around the junk in the yard.

"Far out," Catman said. "You sold many?"

"What?" Dad asked, as if the thought hadn't occurred to him.

"I know a dozen kids who'd beg their parents to buy one of these," Catman said.

"You do?" Dad asked.

Lizzy sprang into action as I pedaled forward to brake, then dropped one foot to the ground.

"Listen to Catman, Dad!" Lizzy begged. "We can't leave here—not when your invention is catching on! Think about it. You could make a bunch of back bikes and sell them at a huge profit! Plus, you'll get more odd jobs once people see what you can do!"

"Spidell might stock the back bike up at A-Mart, if you give him a more-than-fair cut," Catman added.

"Do you really think people around here might buy a back bike?" Dad asked.

"Everybody bikes to school," Catman said. "Being different is in. Backward is cool."

Dad looked right through me and grinned at his bike invention. "I suppose it might be worth a try. . . ."

"*Yes!*" Lizzy shouted. She did another jump that would have sent her sprawling if Catman hadn't reached out to steady her.

"So we're staying?" I asked, afraid to believe it.

Instead of answering me, Dad turned to Catman. "When does school start up around here?"

"About a month," he answered.

"Then we'll give Ohio a month. Pittsburgh will still be there." Dad jogged to the truck and pulled out his suitcases.

"You rock, Catman!" Lizzy exclaimed, throwing her arms around him. I knew she didn't mean anything by it. That was just Lizzy. Then she twirled twice and dashed inside.

I was afraid to look at Catman. I didn't know

why he'd done what he had, after what I'd said about his cats.

"So where are your horses?" he asked.

"We did have horses," I explained, not meeting his gaze. "But we sold them."

"So you're getting more?" he asked, fiddling with the bike chain. "Another horse for your barn?"

Am I getting another horse? Could I, God?

"I'm working on it," I replied.

There was a time when I couldn't tell my thoughts from my prayers. But that had been a long time ago. Lizzy would call Dad's changing his mind another "God thing, grace." Whatever it was, I had another chance. And I'd do everything in my power to buy that Arabian, if it meant working 24 hours a day to earn the money.

Suddenly I had to see her. I wanted to tell the Arabian not to give up, that I wouldn't give up either. And I could start by asking for extra hours at Stable-Mart.

"I have to go," I said.

I hopped on the bike and steered out to the street. I'd rounded the corner before I realized I hadn't even thanked Catman.

To get to Stable-Mart without cutting through

fields, I had to ride down the main street of Ashland. Friday afternoon traffic didn't amount to much, but half a dozen cars eased past me. Nobody seemed to notice I was pedaling backward until I came to a stoplight.

"Look at that kid!" yelled the driver of a banged-up car that pulled beside me. He and his girlfriend looked high school. "No lie! She was pedaling backward!"

I managed to coast to the corner and make a quick right as the light changed, so he couldn't prove his case. Picking up speed downhill, I changed lanes and took the corner at a tilt, trying to get back to the right road.

Straight ahead I saw nothing but clear sailing, a long downhill. Leaning forward over the handlebars, I imagined hugging the neck of my white Arabian as we galloped down a lush, green meadow, with nobody else around, the two of us flying.

Something moved at the side of the road, but sunlight half blinded me. A black dog scurried out in front of me.

"Macho!" shouted a boy running behind the dog. He turned and saw me, but too late. He froze to the middle of the road. Panicked, I hammered the brakes, pumping the pedal back. But that's how normal bikes brake—not a back bike. Faster and faster, I headed straight for the kid and his dog.

Closer and closer. My brain kicked in. I slammed the pedal forward. The brakes screeched. My bike swerved sideways.

And I flew off, crashing smack into the kid.

We rolled down the hill, tangled in the dog's leash. The dog whimpered.

Then we stopped.

"You okay?" the kid asked, unwrapping his dog's leash from my ankle. He was about Lizzy's height, dressed in blue jeans and a yellow T-shirt. He had close-cut, curly black hair and what my mother used to call "colt eyes," big and brown. His skin was the color of a dark bay stallion we used to have.

He reached for his dog, but the skinny creature cringed, as if expecting a blow.

"Don't hit the dog!" I cried. "It wasn't his fault."

"What?" The boy looked confused. "But I—"

I struggled to my feet. If I hadn't worn jeans, I'd have been scraped to pieces.

The dog looked like a war-torn version of a black-and-tan hunting dog we'd had at the ranch.

"Don't be afraid," I said, trying to pet him.

He cowered and whimpered.

How could anybody do this to a dog? I glared at the guy, trying to make *him* cringe.

"I'm really sorry," the kid said. "Macho just took off!"

No wonder!

He laughed. "Good thing you weren't a car. Is your bike okay?"

The back bike had skidded to the side of the road. I ran over and picked it up. It looked to be in one piece. I jumped on before the kid could try to help me. I can't stand to be around anyone who would hurt animals.

"Hey!" he called as I pedaled off. "What's your name? Aren't you pedaling backwards? Maybe your bike's broken!"

I didn't turn around as his voice faded.

I made my way to Stable-Mart. As soon as the huge, white stable came into view, my heart started pounding—not because I'm crazy about that horse factory. The Spidells sell horses like they sell bubble gum in A-Mart or pizza in Pizza-Mart or pets in the giant Pet-Mart on Claremont Avenue. Their stable smells more like a hospital than a barn.

31

But somewhere on those grounds had to be the most beautiful horse in the world—the Arabian Richard called Wild Thing.

I jumped off the still-moving bike and leaned it against a tree. Then I jogged to the south pasture, where I hoped they'd had the good sense to turn out the Arabian. Spidells barely used that pasture, although it was the only one with a natural pond. They didn't want their horses to roll in the mud and get dirty.

I spotted the other auction horses crammed into the paddock, but no Wild Thing. The south pasture lay empty. So did the north pasture. I checked the stable.

Panic seeped into me. *What if they never caught up to the Arabian? What if she ran into a car the same way that frightened dog ran into my bike?*

From outside the stable came a squeal that shuddered through me as if I'd made it myself. Horses only make that high-pitched whine out of pure terror.

And I knew in my bones the cry came from Wild Thing.

In spite of the heat, I shivered as I raced through the stable toward the horrible cry.

In a corner of the training pen stood the proud Arabian, tied short to a post as thick as a telephone pole. A black hood covered her head.

"Keep away from Wild Thing!" somebody yelled behind me.

I didn't turn. I couldn't breathe.

She'd been rigged so she couldn't put her hind leg down. A chain ran from the pole, through the D ring of her halter, all the way back to her right hind leg.

I saw the mare's leg twitch backward, as if to kick at the contraption. Her head bobbed, and she winced as the chain's roping action tugged the halter, inflicting pain.

"I said keep away!" Richard shouted.

I wheeled on him. "How could you . . . ?"
I spit out the words, fighting back tears that
burned in my throat. "How could you do that?"

"Are you kidding?" Richard said. "That horse
is crazy!"

The mare snorted and tried to rear, but her
forelegs were hobbled together—with two
leather bracelets connected by a short chain.

Richard scurried back. "We're not hurting
the horse. It's what Dad calls 'self-inflicted
pain.' If the stupid horse doesn't act up, she's
fine."

I'd heard all about that kind of horse-break-
ing. My mom had had a reputation as a horse
gentler. She believed in loving horses—not
breaking their spirits.

"You *and* your dad should just—!" I bit the
inside of my cheek to stop myself. Richard
Spidell would as soon fire me as spit. Then
where would that leave Wild Thing?

I took a deep breath and counted to four.

"Um . . . Richard, why the hood? She's got to
hate total darkness. It'll just make her wilder."

"I tried to put her in blinders instead. Look
what I got for my trouble." He lifted his T-shirt

to show me the faint outline of two teeth marks just above his waist.

I tried not to smile. *Way to go, Wild Thing!*

I glanced at Richard, who's nearly six feet tall and a junior in high school. Lizzy says he looks like a Wild West movie star, but I don't see it. Lizzy also says *I* look like Annie Oakley, the famous Wild West cowgirl.

"Dad left me in charge of Wild Thing after six of us got her hobbled," Richard griped. He frowned at the mare as she hopped on three legs to keep her balance.

"How am I supposed to get that wild beast into a stall?" he whined. "And Dad expects *me* to find out how old she is? That auctioneer sold her blind-age. Nobody could get near her mouth."

I could feel Wild Thing's fear. I had to do something. "Richard," I said, trying to sound as people-friendly as my sister does, "if you get that sack off her head, she'll calm down. She needs to see what she's up against. I could help."

He snorted a laugh. "You?"

I forced a casual smile. "I've always had this weird connection with horses." Mom used to say I connected because I had good horse sense. Dad used to say he wished I had people sense.

Richard took off his cowboy hat and frowned. "You get hurt, they'll blame me."

"I won't get hurt," I said, trying not to sound excited. "And if I do, I'll say you tried to stop me."

Richard twisted his lips. I could tell he didn't think I could do it, but he was out of options.

"And," I added, "I'll find out how old she is."

That clinched it. He glanced over his shoulder. Nobody was around. "Okay. But be careful! That mare's a hothead."

The Arabian was no hothead. I hated that she'd gotten the name Wild Thing. I slipped through the gate, checking to make sure Richard didn't try to come in after me. He didn't.

The smell of fear nearly gagged me, but I knew most humans couldn't even smell it. She smelled me, too, her nostrils flaring beneath the black mask. She tried to paw, but the hobbles at her forelegs made her stumble.

"Easy, girl," I said, my heart twitching like her skin. "It's just me, Winnie. Remember?"

She snorted.

I moved to her head, shuffling in the dust so she'd hear me approach. I kept up a slow stream of nonsense: "Now isn't this a fine mess they've put you into. We'll have to see what we can do to train these silly humans."

Inches from her head, I blew at her nostrils. It's an old Native American trick Mom taught me, a horse-to-horse greeting. I waited for her to return the favor. Her neck arched, the tendons and muscles quivering.

"Careful!" Richard shouted.

I ignored him and hoped the mare would too. I blew again.

This time she snorted her greeting.

"So you *are* glad to see me," I said, edging my hand up until I could get a good hold on the black silk hood. I eased it up and off. "Let there be light," I said, knowing it was a Bible verse, feeling it was a prayer.

The mare whinnied and tried to buck. But the back hobble wouldn't let her, and the chain jerked her head.

Blaming me for the pain, she bared her teeth, flattened her ears back, and tried to bite. I jumped out of the way just in time.

"That's enough!" Richard yelled. "She'll kill you!"

"I'm fine," I called back. "I know her age—at least four, maybe five."

Thanks to her biting maneuver, I'd gotten a good look at her teeth. I hadn't had time to count and see if she had all 36 teeth, but her milk teeth were gone.

"Are you sure?" Richard asked.

"I'm sure," I said. "She has her lateral permanent incisors, which they get at four years. Okay? And I saw her corner incisors. They come down about a year later in mares. I'd say she's five."

No way was I going to cram her into a Spidell stall, where she'd become one of the cogs in their horse factory. I had to convince Richard to turn her out in the pasture.

"Richard," I said, "I'd be afraid to take her into the stalls. She might kick her way out. How about the south pasture?"

Richard didn't like the idea. But finally he gave up.

I reached for the back hobble to unhook the chain. Wild Thing's ears went back, and her neck craned around. She was thinking about biting me.

"No thanks," I said, politely pressing her head back around.

Again I squatted to unhook the hobble. And again came the head, ears flat back in fighting mode.

"No thanks," I said, reaching up and gently pressing her head back. Seven or eight more times Wild Thing reached her head around. Each time, I played along and pressed her head back gently.

Richard sighed loudly, letting me know he wasn't enjoying this.

Patience is a horsewoman's best friend, I thought, remembering one of Mom's favorite lines.

Finally when I reached for her hind hoof, the mare sighed and didn't object. I unfastened the back hobble and the front straps with no problem.

Wild Thing's halter, though, was hopelessly tangled in the lead chain. While I ran one hand under her mane to her crest, I unbuckled the halter with the other. Gently clutching a handful of her poll, the top lock of hair at the highest part of the mane, I let the halter slip off.

"She'll run away!" Richard shouted.

"Easy, girl," I said, ignoring Richard. With my left hand at her poll, I wrapped my right hand across the bridge of her nose, above the nostrils.

Standing at her shoulder, I took a step forward. She moved out with me. Her eyes showed too much white, and she still smelled of fear, but she followed me to the pasture. I made sure we were well into the pasture before I took my hands away.

The mare bolted, twisted in midair, and took off at a dead gallop, her tail high as freedom's flag.

Richard let me out, then double-checked the gate latch. "I don't know how you did it, but you did. Good job!"

Job! There would never be a better time to hit Richard up for what I really needed now—a real job.

"You think I did a good job?" I asked. We leaned on the gate and looked out to where Wild Thing pranced against the dusk, the orange-gray clouds swirling in the sky behind her.

"Unless you were just making that up about her age," he said.

"No, she's about five."

"Great." He put his hat back on.

I plunged in. "The reason I'm asking if you like the *job* I did is because I need one."

"You already have a job here, Winnie."

"Mucking stalls. I want to help with the horses, Richard. I need the money. I could train Wild Thing *and* keep the mucking job."

Richard scraped his snakeskin boots on the

bottom rung of the gate. "I just hire stablehands. Dad hires trainers."

"But you could put in a good word for me!" I insisted. "Tell him how I handled Wild Thing?"

"Maybe." He tucked in his checkered shirt. "Dad's set on making a profit off that horse."

"Then you'll—?" I started.

"There you are!" Spider Spidell shouted. People call Richard's dad Spider because his arms reach all over Ashland with his businesses. But he reminded me more of a blue jay than a spider. A stubborn rim of dark hair clung to his otherwise bald head, sticking out in a point in back, like a jay's. Thick, dark eyebrows met in angry peaks above tiny eyes.

"I've been looking all over for you!" he shouted again, even though he'd stormed up to within inches of us.

Then Mr. Spidell seemed to notice me for the first time. Transforming into a kindly stable owner, he stuck out his hand. "I don't believe I've had the pleasure. Are you boarding your horse with us?"

"Winnie works for us, Dad," Richard explained. "She cleans the stalls twice a day."

"Ah," he said, dropping the nice-man routine

and loosening his tie. "Those buyers left without seeing that Arabian. They lost interest when I couldn't even tell them how old she is."

"But I can tell you, Dad!" Richard said eagerly. "She's five. Well, almost five anyway."

His dad frowned at him. "It's rare for such a young Arabian to be so white already. Are you making this up?"

Richard licked his lips. "Her . . . um . . . teeth . . ."

"Her lateral incisors are all the way in, and the corner ones are just about to size," I said.

"Yeah," Richard agreed.

"Hmm . . . then she *is* about five," Mr. Spidell commented. "And white like that . . . that's good. Nice work, Richard."

Richard smiled nervously.

I gritted my teeth, waiting for him to tell his dad about me.

"So where is the beast?" Mr. Spidell asked. "I didn't see her in the stalls."

"I thought she'd do better if we let her run in the pasture," Richard said.

You *thought she should run in the pasture?* I didn't like the way this was going. *Come on! Tell him about me, Richard!*

"You're probably right," his dad said, staring out at the Arabian. "She's a beauty though, isn't she? But how on earth did you get her out here all by yourself?"

Yeah, Richard, I thought, trying to get his attention. *How did you get her out here? Tell him! Tell him he needs to hire me!*

"Ah," Richard said, turning his back on me, "it wasn't that hard."

Richard's dad put an arm around his son's shoulder. "Maybe there's hope for you yet, boy."

I stared numbly after them as they walked toward the stable. Richard didn't give me so much as a glance over his shoulder.

So much for my "good job." Thanks a lot, Richard.

I started evening mucking early, stabbing the spade into piles of manure. Harder and faster I scooped and heaved until sweat poured down my neck. I hated the scrape of the spade on the cement stall floors just under the shredded rubber covering. At our ranch in Wyoming, Mom insisted on straw flooring clean enough to eat off of.

I dug in harder, every muscle exploding with anger. *How could Richard Spidell take credit for handling the Arabian?*

When I'd filled the wheelbarrow, I pushed it to the stallway and hoisted the manure onto the dump wagon. Mornings I worked the north stalls, evenings the south.

I'd left the end stall for last, Scar's stall. That

was my name for Summer Spidell's high-strung American Saddle Horse. The name on the gold plate tacked on the stall door read Spidell's Sophisticated Scarlet Lady. I imagine they got the *Scarlet* from the mare's reddish roan coat.

Scarlet, Scar, was the only horse who refused to make up to me. From all the pictures of Summer holding trophies and ribbons, her horse was good for horse shows but not much else.

I couldn't blame the mare. As I raked her stall, Scar was taking up space in a hot walker, a contraption like a playground merry-go-round, without seats or fun. Spokes radiate from a center pole, like one of Dad's bike wheels on its side. When owners don't care enough to ride their horses, they stick them in the hot walker for exercise.

Poor Scar circled round and round, her ears lopped in boredom.

Dumping my last load into the manure wagon, I noticed that the stall across from Scar's had both the top and bottom doors closed. It was bad enough that Spidells held horses prisoners in their stalls day and night. But top halves of stall doors were usually left open so the horses could at least see other four-legged creatures.

This stall belonged to a sweet-natured Appaloosa, who always hung around while I cleaned his horse-prison "cell." I'd never been in that stall when the gelding wasn't. Solid brown in front, with a white rump dotted with brown-ish-black spots, he would have made a perfect example of the horses known as Palousa, prized spotted horses of the Nez Perce Indians, who broke away from the Palouse tribe in Idaho.

I glanced both ways. A little girl was brushing her horse five stalls away. Half a dozen horses trudged in hot walkers. A handful of ponies jogged around a small arena, their riders intent on posture and form.

Nobody was looking.

I crossed the stallway and pushed back the top door. The Appaloosa let out a grateful nicker. As I slid inside the stall, he turned toward me.

I gasped. "You poor baby!"

Someone had put a mechanical cribber, a wide leather strap that latches tightly around a horse's throat, on that beautiful animal. And this cribber looked like one of the cruelest styles, with a small, metal spike sticking out of the strap. Horses will sometimes grab the top of a board of their stall with their front teeth and chew, and a cribber is designed to prevent the horse from arching his neck enough to reach over the wood and inhale. The first day I worked at Stable-Mart, I'd noticed several stall boards gnawed at the top—sure signs of cribbing. In some cases, the horse goes one step further and gulps air while chewing. It's called wind sucking. It's not good for the horse, and it's not good for the stall.

But no horse deserved what they'd done to the Appy.

He walked toward me, nodding a greeting. I saw him wince as he stretched out his neck and a small metal spike poked him in the throat. There was no need for that spike! The strap alone would have kept the horse from cribbing.

Anger flashed in me like a struck match. I reached up and unbuckled the strap, letting it drop to the ground. It landed in a fresh mound of horse droppings.

"Good place for it, huh, boy?" I said, rubbing his outstretched neck.

I eyed the cribber covered with manure. "Looks to me as if your stall needs cleaning." I scooped up manure with the spade. The cribber "just happened" to come along. *Next stop—the manure wagon.*

With the spade braced in front of me, I leaned my back against the stall door, pushing it open again.

"Winifred, what are you doing in there?" Summer Spidell frowned down at me as if I were making snowmen out of the mess instead of shoveling it.

"What's it look like I'm doing?" I asked, hoping she wouldn't study my shovelful and see the cribber.

Summer would probably be in some of my classes if we stayed in Ashland until school started.

Mom used to say, "Winnie, there are owners who love horses as friends. And there are owners who show horses for the applause it brings the rider." I'd known two minutes after I saw Summer with her horse which kind of owner she was.

"Weren't you supposed to clean this stall in the morning?" she asked, smoothing the blonde hair that flowed over her shoulders as if it weren't a thousand degrees in the shade.

"I did," I said truthfully, keeping my body

between Summer and the spade. "But whoever owns this gelding sure doesn't take care of the stall. And I can't stand to think of the Appy standing in muck all night. So if you'll excuse me . . ."

I sidled around the door, keeping my back to Summer. If I could just pitch the load . . .

I hauled back for all I was worth, ready to fire into the muck wagon.

"Squawk! Hello? Who's there?"

The screeching, unearthly voice made me jerk my arm. It threw off my aim. The spade flew upward, and the manure rained down—down onto Summer Spidell.

"Help! Help me!" Summer screamed, as if she were drowning in quicksand. She slapped her lavender shorts and top, although only a couple of clumps had actually stuck.

"Sorry," I said, trying not to laugh.

"You're going to be!" Summer snapped.

"Help! Help me!"

This time I spotted the mimic. Behind Summer stood a tall, slender girl with straight, shiny black hair that parted in the middle and hung down to her waist. On her shoulder sat the brightest red bird I'd ever seen. It was a foot long, counting the red tail, with bright green-and-yellow wings.

"Help! Help me! Uh-oh!" it squawked.

"What is that?" I asked. I'd never seen anything like it.

"This is an Indonesian breed of parrot—the talking bird of the sun and dawn," said the girl, who could have passed for an exotic Native American princess. "It is called a chattering lory. His name is Peter."

She didn't crack a grin. Her words came out one at a time, almost too clear, as if they'd been cut from ice.

Summer was still shaking her hair and stomping her sandaled feet. "Did you see this idiot throw Towaco's manure all over me?"

"I didn't—," I started to protest. "Towaco? Is that the Appaloosa's name? Well, if Towaco's owner cared anything about him, none of this would have happened!"

Summer sneered, as if she'd just gotten me in trouble with the principal. "Allow me to introduce you to Towaco's owner," she said, pointing to the dark-haired girl. "Victoria Hawkins, as in *Hawkins and Hawkins Attorneys at Law.*"

Summer pointed at me. "This is Winifred

something. She works for my father cleaning stalls—although after today—"

"Summer," Victoria interrupted, "you said the spike on that cribber would never touch my horse." She paused, easily peering over my head into the stall. "Where's the strap? I thought we had to leave the cribber on."

Summer stormed around me to look for herself. "We do have to leave it on!" Then as if she'd just noticed the stall's top door, she asked, "Why is this door open? And where is that cribber?" She wheeled on me. "What do *you* know about this?"

I'd probably lost my job already. Anger relit, so real I felt it knife behind my eyeballs. "I took that stupid cribber off!" I shouted, kicking it out of the manure.

"Who gave you the right—?" Summer screamed, scurrying out of the way.

"Towaco!" I shouted back at her. "That's who! Couldn't you see his pain?" My throat felt raw, as if *I* were wearing the cribber and stretching my neck out too far. Maybe I was. But I couldn't help it. "How could anyone who even pretends to like horses use that thing?" I asked.

"You are so ignorant," Summer said. "It's for the horse's own good."

I kicked at the cribber again, splattering up straw and muck. "Own good? Then *you* wear it!"

Summer faked a smile to Victoria Hawkins, who hadn't so much as blinked during the shouting match. "Winifred doesn't realize cribbing is catching. We can't have our entire stable chewed to the ground."

It was all I could do not to shove her face-first into the manure wagon. "Cribbing isn't a virus!" I cried. "Horses don't catch it!"

Summer's gray eyes narrowed like she knew she had me now. "Then how do you explain the fact that half of our horses chew on the stalls?" She folded her arms in front of her.

"How do I explain it?" I demanded, stepping closer, forcing Summer to take a step back. "Easy! They're all cooped up like Towaco! They hate Stable-Mart! What else is there to do in here? *I'd* chew wood if you locked me up here! They're *bored!*" I pushed past Summer and almost slammed into Victoria and her bird.

"Bored! Bored! Bored!" squawked the parrot.

"Well, at least one of you has a brain," I muttered, storming down the stallway to the nearest exit.

"Don't bother coming back!" Summer yelled after me. "I'm telling Daddy to fire you!"

Not until I got outside and inhaled the dusky air did it hit me. *Fired?* I'd just lost my job.

Without the trainer's job, maybe I never would have had the Arabian anyway. I would have had to muck a lot of stalls to buy the mare. But at least I could have stayed close to her. I could have seen her morning and night. I could have looked out for her.

Now I didn't even have that.

I hadn't just lost my job. I'd lost the Arabian. And it felt like losing everything all over again.

A loneliness burned in my chest as I ran to the south pasture. I had to see Wild Thing one more time.

She was racing the wind at the back fence. With her neck stretched into the sunset, she looked like she might jump into the sky. For an instant I pictured my mom riding the Arabian bareback across heaven.

Suddenly the mare tossed her silvery mane, slid to a stop, and craned her neck in my direction.

She saw me. I knew she did.

I would have given anything to hear her nicker. A nicker is the warmest, friendliest greeting in the world. I could almost have stood not seeing her again if only I could hear her nicker.

"Hey, Winnie!" Richard Spidell joined me at

the gate. "Think we can catch her—like in a couple of days?"

"You're asking *me?*" I said sarcastically.

"Come on," Richard said in a mushy voice that probably worked with most girls. "We could work together."

I turned to glare at him. "Don't they tell you anything? I won't be around. Your sister fired me."

"Summer?" he asked, his forehead wrinkling.

"That's the one," I answered.

"She can't do that," he said.

"Well she did."

"No. I mean, she *can't* fire you . . . or anybody. *I* hire barn labor." Richard put an arm around my shoulder.

I scowled at him until he removed it. "So she'll tell your dad to fire me," I said. "Same difference."

"No way!" Richard insisted. "When it comes to Stable-Mart and the horses, Summer doesn't tell Dad anything. It just starts a fight. Dad wants her to show English *and* Western, but she won't do it. She loves decking out in her English riding habit, posting on that American Saddle Horse. If she shows Western, she's afraid she'll look like a cowboy. But Dad's determined to get her into Western classes in the fall horse shows. Trust me. Summer's not about to bring up horses *or* you with Dad."

Hope tingled through me like electricity. "Don't just say this stuff, Richard," I warned.

He crossed his heart. "I promise! You're not fired."

"I'm not fired?" I repeated, letting it sink in.

He shook his head. "What would I do without my best mucker?"

I was practically his only mucker, and I knew it. Some ninth-grade guy came in on the week-ends, but mostly I was it.

"So . . ." He started to put his hand on my shoulder, then jerked it back. "You'll keep clean-ing stalls. And you can help me catch Wild Thing when I need to?"

I'm back! Did you do this, God? If you did, thanks.

I stared out at the Arabian. The sun had set, leaving the mare a dark shadow under the oak tree.

"See you tomorrow," I said.

"Great!" Richard said, walking off.

But I'd said it to the Arabian. "Good night, Wild Thing!"

I waited for her returning nicker, imagined it, prayed for it.

It didn't come.

But I still had my job. True, Lizzy earned more babysitting than I did at hard labor in those stalls. I'd still need to get a second job to earn money to buy Wild Thing. But for the time being, I was grateful knowing I could still keep an eye on her.

That night after a great "Lizzy dinner" of tuna casserole and Waldorf salad, I dreamed of our ranch in Wyoming. The barns looked the same in memory snapshots that played even while I was asleep. But in my dream, the pastures were filled with hundreds of white Arabians.

In the morning I pulled on Levi's and one of Lizzy's clean T-shirts before the sun had time to rise. Still, I didn't make it out before my sister. Her bed looked like it hadn't been slept in.

I flipped on our light so I could dig under my bed. I'd managed to keep one thing of Mom's through all our moves—a faded green saddle blanket. I pulled out my suitcase, opened it, and took out the blanket. Mom had loved riding bareback. But if she saddled up, she'd use this blanket. It still smelled like her old buckskin mare.

Sticking the blanket under my arm, I kicked my suitcase back under the bed with the rest of my stuff.

Even though I hadn't unpacked my clothes, my dresser drawers hung open, making empty stairsteps. Blank walls backed my unmade bed. Stacks of books and horse magazines piled up everywhere, spilling into Lizzy's space.

Lizzy's side of our room looked like a page out of her teen magazines. Her clothes were folded in dresser drawers she never left open. Frilly pillow covers matched her blue bedspread and the poster of the world's largest gecko lizard. Her wall held pictures in neat, blue frames.

Above the light switch, Lizzy had hung the two framed needlepoint projects she and Mom had done together days before the accident. Mom had used fancy crewelwork stitching and little threaded knots to outline her favorite verse from the Bible. Perfectly formed blue letters declared:

For your unfailing love is as high as the heavens. Your faithfulness reaches to the clouds.

—PSALM 57:10

Next to Mom's frame was the one Lizzy had attempted. It wasn't half bad, considering she'd only been nine. Lizzy's red stitches looked simple next to Mom's.

The first part came right from the Bible. But Lizzy had gotten tired of the project and shortened the end of her verse:

> God in his gracious kindness declares us
>   not guilty.
> Jesus didn't die for nothing!

Mom had laughed so hard when she'd read it, she'd almost choked. No amount of prodding could make Lizzy finish off the project by embroidering where the verse came from. I remembered, though, because Lizzy had left her Bible open with a red box around Romans 3:24. My mind had taken one of its long-lasting photos.

My stomach growled me into action. Dad's bedroom was off the kitchen, and I heard him snoring as I poured myself grape juice. Lizzy must have fried sausage patties really early since they were totally cooled in the skillet. I took one, bit a mouthful, and headed outside with the blanket still under my arm.

The air felt cool, and a couple of stars were

holding out in the black sky. I smelled asters and field mustard as I started down the porch steps. I could still see the two framed needlework verses in my head. Lizzy's red letters pressed behind my eyelids: *God in his gracious kindness declares us not guilty.*

Right! I thought. *Like my little sister has anything to feel guilty about. That's* my *department.*

"Careful!" Lizzy called.

I'd stepped off the porch and nearly landed on her back.

She was squatted in the bushes below the porch.

"Lizzy!" I cried. "What are you—?"

"Look who's back!" she whispered, pointing to the poplar tree next to the house.

I looked, but I couldn't see anything.

"Larry!" she said, creeping to the tree. Her index finger moved to the bark and stroked something.

That's when I saw her lizard. This time I could make out the blue ring on his neck.

"That's amazing!" I said.

"I knew Larry would come back," Lizzy explained, "especially if I tempted him with my homemade bug-burger."

Bug-burger? I spit out my mouthful of sausage. Suddenly it tasted like cockroaches.

"Lizzy!" I cried, spitting and choking. "How could you leave bug-burgers out on the stove?"

"These are bug-burgers." She held up a mound of bumpy brown that looked more like a big bug with mumps than a sausage patty. *"Those—"* she motioned with her head toward the house— "are sausage patties."

"I knew that," I said, wiping the corners of my mouth. My stomach still felt like bugs were crawling around inside.

Lizzy placed one of her burgers in the crook of a branch above her lizard. "Larry will bring his friends around. Wouldn't that rock, Winnie?"

In Wyoming, Lizzy had had her own ranch—a lizard ranch. She'd lured so many lizards to her menagerie that our elementary school ran field trips there. In the few months we'd lived in Iowa, Lizzy had put together a bug farm.

"If anybody can round up lizards in Ohio, Lizzy, you're the one," I declared, pitching the rest of my sausage into the bushes.

"I almost forgot!" Lizzy exclaimed, turning her attention to a fist-sized hole she was digging with her bare hands just under the tree. I didn't ask why. "Catman's in the barn."

My heart sped up, then slowed back down. *So what? What do I care? That kid is weird.*

"Is Catman helping you with the lizard collection?" I asked, pretending to yawn.

"Nah," Lizzy said. "I've decided, Winnie. You can have him." She said it like we were divvying up marbles.

"Huh?" I asked.

"Catman," she answered simply. "You can have Catman. Not that he isn't the cutest guy since Illinois. Or was it Indiana? Remember Bryan in that school with the red clocks? I think that's when we lived above the martial arts studio—"

"What *are* you talking about?" I interrupted.

"Catman! As cute as he is, he's not my type."

My sister, my *little* sister, had a *type?*

"Elizabeth Priscilla Willis," I began. At least Lizzy had the good sense to flinch when I pulled out her hated middle name. "You're 11 years old! You can't have a *type!*"

Lizzy smiled over her shoulder at me, as if she were 111 years old. "Winnie, Winnie . . . you have a lot to learn about male humans."

I had a lot to learn about my *little* sister.

"I'm *so* outta here!" I said, grabbing the back bike and balancing the green horse blanket across the handlebars.

"I'll tell Catman you said hello!" Lizzy shouted as I pedaled out to the street.

"Don't you dare!" I shouted back.

Even Stable-Mart horses are easier to understand than humans! Arabians are my type. Morgans and Quarter Horses are my type. I can't think of a horse that isn't my type.

But boys? No idea.

Chapter

1

*M*y first morning glimpse of Wild Thing stopped my heart. She looked even more gorgeous in the morning light.

Thanks, God, I prayed, as I walked to the fence. *I know I haven't had much to say lately. But only you could make a horse this incredible.*

I tried to think of something else to say. But prayer didn't feel natural anymore. *That's all. Amen.*

I tossed the blanket over the fence and ducked between railings, catching my hair in the splintered wood. I hadn't taken time to braid my hair, so it fell in waves past my shoulders. I yanked the strand free. "Morning, girl!"

She snorted, watching my every step.

"You can give me a nicker if you want to," I suggested.

She didn't want to.

Mid-pasture, still a good distance from the Arabian, I spread out the horse blanket onto the wet grass and plopped down cross-legged.

Wild Thing didn't know what to think. She tossed her head and let out a warning whinny.

But I sat still. *"Wild Thing.* Now what kind of a name is that for such a beautiful horse? There must be a thousand names that suit you better."

In fact, I'd been shoving names away from my mind ever since I'd seen the Arabian.

"At our ranch," I explained, "Mom and I got too attached to the horses we took on to gentle. So we made a rule: No naming unless the horse is a keeper."

The mare's long neck stretched as she reached up and lipped a broad, green leaf from the tree.

"You are definitely a keeper," I went on. "And I'm going to do everything I can to make sure I'm the one doing the keeping. But until then, no naming."

I visited with Wild Thing until the sun was fully up. She never came closer, but eventually felt at ease enough to graze. And when I left the pasture, she lifted her head and watched.

After mucking, I biked home. Catman and Dad were huddled around a silver funnel that had wires coming out of it. In cutoffs and a black shirt with a peace emblem on the front, Catman still looked like he'd stepped out of a hippie antiwar protest.

"Back bike's back," Catman announced.

"It is?" Dad glanced up, seeming to see the bike but not me.

"Me too," I said, trying to act like not being noticed was funny.

"Hello, Winnie." Dad gathered the funnel thing, a metal band, and a handful of screws.

When we lived on the ranch in Wyoming, Dad used to rush off to his office in Laramie before the school bus came. Sometimes when he got home, Lizzy and I had already gone to bed. Mom used to tell us that Dad peeked in on us. I believed her then. But I'm not sure he did. I'd have bet money he hadn't peeked in on me since the accident. Who could blame him?

"Morning, Dad," I said, staring at his work boots.

"Bring the bike over here, will you, Winnie?"

Dad asked. "I've received three orders for bikes already! Friends of Catman's."

"That's great, Dad." I wheeled the bike over, not glancing up at Catman. "Where's Lizzy?"

"Lizzy?" Dad repeated.

"My sister?"

He dropped a screw, picked it up. "Baby-sitting for the Barkers."

Lizzy got the job three days after we'd moved in. That's how great she is with people. From what I remembered, Lizzy watched a couple of the Barker kids while their mom or dad ran others to music lessons or something. I hadn't met any of them yet.

I needed Lizzy to help me find a second job. She already knew every business in Ashland. "When will she be home?" I asked.

"Uh-oh." Dad patted his pockets. "Pliers." He trotted off toward the garage, then hollered back, "Thanks for your help, Catman!"

Catman narrowed his Siamese-cat eyes at me. "Lizzy said you need a job. You like any animals besides horses?"

"I love all animals!" I protested.

"Good. Come on." He took off, hands behind his back as if handcuffed.

"Come? Where?" I asked, jogging to keep up.

Catman didn't turn around. "I know the woman who runs the pet store."

"Seriously?" A pet-store job would be perfect. Then I remembered who owned the pet store. "The Spidells won't hire me. Summer and I don't exactly get along."

"Not Pet-Mart," he said. "Pat's Pets, over on Second."

We cut through the pasture behind the house and across a field.

"Mind if I stop by my house?" Catman asked. "Need to pick up something."

"Sure," I said, hurrying to keep up with his long strides.

When we crossed a creek, I thought, *One day Wild Thing and I will splash across this creek.*

If Lizzy had been in my place, she would already have given Catman our whole history. He probably would have opened up to her too. Most people do.

But Catman and I trekked on to the sounds of cracking twigs, cawing birds, and my footsteps. *He* was catlike quiet.

Two orange tabby cats pranced out of the

bushes to greet Catman. They rubbed against his ankles and fell in with us.

"Hey, Wilhemina," he cooed, scratching the fattest cat, fat enough to be having kittens.

"You named your cat Wilhemina?" I asked, grinning.

"Right-on," he said, petting the larger, orange cat until she purred. "Charles Dickens—wrote *David Copperfield* and *Tale of Two Cities*—loved his cat. Called him William until the cat had kittens. Changed to Wilhemina."

"How about that one?" I asked, pointing to the smaller, light orange cat purring at his ankles.

"Moggie," he said. "That's what the English call a nonpedigree cat. I rescued this one from a pond. Somebody tried to drown the whole litter."

He started off again, the cats weaving between his sandals. Catman veered off the path to an overgrown lane lined with vine-twisted trees.

Another cat jumped from the bushes, scaring the breath out of me.

"Burg!" Catman called.

The longhaired, white cat crept to him, not

rushing as the other cats had. Its eyes were ringed with black, like a mask.

"Burg?" I asked, trying to pet the cat. But he darted off.

"Cat Burglar," he answered.

The lane ended in a patch of weeds. I looked up to see a run-down house on a hill, worthy of any ghost story I'd ever read. Gables poked out of a battered roof. Some of the windows had boards hammered over them.

"Wow!" I said, gawking at the monster mansion. "Spooky. Do kids come here on Halloween?"

I thought I saw Catman grin, but it vanished before I could be sure. *"I* do," he said.

"How long has this place been deserted?" I asked.

He didn't answer, but made his way through the tall grass up the hill.

The house had to be at least three stories tall, and the whole house needed a coat of paint bad. If I'd had the nerve, I would have asked him to skip *this* shortcut.

Instead of ducking around the house, Catman headed straight for the porch, all three cats at his heels.

"What are you doing?" I whispered.

He climbed the porch steps.

"Catman! Don't go in!"

He reached for the screen door and called back, "Coming?"

I didn't want him to think I was a scared little kid, so I tiptoed up the stairs. They squeaked. I shivered.

Catman opened the door. The cats scurried in ahead of him.

"Now what are you going to do?" I asked, trying to keep the terror out of my voice—and failing. "Kitty? Kitty?" I whispered. "Catman, we can't just leave them in there!"

I imagined vampire bats swooping down on the cats.

"It's cool." Catman slipped inside and held the door open, leaving me no choice.

It took a minute for my eyes to get used to the dark. When they did, I couldn't believe how beautiful everything looked. The living room was the size of a gym, but velvet furniture and tapestry wall coverings made it feel homey. A huge couch and maybe a dozen chairs and lamps seemed new, but looked as if they'd been shipped from another century.

"Let's go!" I whispered. "Somebody's living here!"

Catman grinned. He leaned over and picked up a cat, a different cat—huge, with short gray hair and a funny face, flat as a silver dollar.

"How's my Churchill?" Catman asked it.

Churchill?

"Calvin! There you are!" A woman waved down at us from the top of a spiral staircase.

Calvin?

Catman waved back. "Hey, Mom."

Chapter 8

I stared stupidly up the staircase at the chubby woman clomping down. Her deep yellow hair was wound around juice-can curlers. With each step, green slippers peeked out of her fuzzy, red bathrobe.

She rushed down to us. "How wonderful to meet a friend of Calvin's!"

"Mom, this is Winnie," he said softly.

Out of the corner of my eye, I glimpsed a sea of multicolored fur closing in on us. Cats crept from under footstools and on top of tables. Cats poured from secret rooms, hissing, competing for Catman's attention.

Calvin's mother gasped and fingered my hair. "Natural curl! Thick and shiny! There's not a girl at my salon who wouldn't *kill* for hair like this!"

I made a mental note never to go to her salon.

She whisked off her glasses as if she'd just realized she was wearing them. "I could fix those split ends, dear."

"Thanks," I muttered. *Could I be more embarrassed?*

"Sa-a-ay," bellowed a man wrestling with his Tweety Bird tie as he crossed the room. "Aren't you the girl who pedals her bicycle backward?"

So, okay. I could *get more embarrassed.*

"Sa-a-ay, how do you do that? Why, if I sold cars that went backward, where would I be?" He shook my hand hard. "Bart Coolidge of Smart Bart's Used Cars! You drive 'em, we sell 'em, you drive 'em again! Ever heard of me?"

I shook my head.

He looked disappointed.

Cats continued to close in—big, little, black, white, gray, orange, brown.

"Be right back," Catman said, handing me a tiny black cat with one white paw. He leaped the banister and zoomed upstairs. Cats scampered after him.

I stroked the kitty's head, wishing Catman would hurry back.

"That's Nelson," Mrs. Coolidge offered, "from Churchill and Wilhemina's last litter."

"The boy says Winston Churchill had a cat named Nelson," Mr. Coolidge explained. "Helped the big man win the war."

The kitten purred, a rattling hum, then sneezed.

Mr. Coolidge patted his hairpiece as if it were his pet cat. "Why did the chicken cross the road?" he asked me.

I laughed, even without the punch line. Something about Bart Coolidge grew on you. "I don't know," I answered.

"To get to Smart Bart's Used Cars so he could drive for a change!" He laughed in windy huffs that sounded like neighs.

I laughed too.

Catman slid down the banister, a notebook between his teeth. "E-mails," he said when he'd spit out the notebook.

As we left, Catman pointed at his herd of cats. "Stay."

They mewed. They waved their tails and circled. But not one made a move to follow us until it was too late and we were on the other side of the closed door.

We left by another path. "Th-they're nice,"

I stammered, feeling guilty for thinking his house was haunted. "I wish we had a house that big."

"Best pad we've had," he said.

I followed Catman through an empty lot that ended at a brick building just off Main Street. I'd passed it before but thought it was a regular house. Now that I took a better look, I could see the faded white letters on the picture window: Pat's Pets.

I pressed my nose to the glass and peered inside. Three puppies yapped and pounced the glass. A row of cages lined one wall. One corner had been turned into a dog pen. Another had a desk and computer. Pat's Pets still looked more like a home than a pet store.

Maybe this would be the answer to my problem. If I could work here, I could earn the money for Wild Thing fast!

Catman walked on in.

I started to follow when I heard a yelp. I turned to see a puppy tied to the bushes—the same abused dog I'd almost run over. "What has your mean master done to you?" I asked, reaching to pet him.

He cringed.

Furious, I stormed into the pet store, ready to give that kid a piece of my mind.

"That's Winnie," Catman said. He was towering over a woman who looked as old as my dad and couldn't have been much taller than me. Short brown curls bounced around her round face and big brown eyes, and her smile showed half her teeth. She wore a fringed, Western vest over a green-checkered shirt and blue jeans.

"Winnie!" she exclaimed, as if we were old friends who hadn't seen each other for years. I knew right away she was like Lizzy—an instant friend to everyone she ran across.

"Winnie . . . what?" she asked.

"Winnie Willis," I answered.

"No!" she said, as if I'd just revealed something huge. "You're Lizzy's sister!"

I nodded.

"I wondered when I'd get to meet you. Your dad is a genius. Already fixed two aquarium pumps I thought were dead in the water. Well, I'll be a monkey's uncle! No offense," she said quickly, scanning the pet store. "Oops. Forgot. Gave that monkey to the Cleveland Zoo. So how's the house working out?"

"Okay," I said, confused.

"Pat owns your house and barn," Catman explained.

"You're Mrs. Haven?" I asked. I'd never met our landlady.

"Call me Pat!" she said. "I insist. Mrs. Haven was my mother-in-law! Lizzy said you were terrific with horses. My husband—God rest his soul—raised horses right in your backyard. Now, what can I do you for?"

Pat Haven talked almost as fast as Lizzy. I glanced at Catman, but he was leaving this to me. "Can I have a job?"

Great sales pitch, Winnie! Maybe Smart Bart's will hire you to sell used cars.

"Well, rats! No offense." Pat nodded at the white mice cages. "To tell the ugly truth, Winnie, I'm barely getting by here. Can't afford to pay myself. Pet-Mart is running me out of business."

Spidells again. It wasn't fair. Why should *they* run the whole town—*and* own Wild Thing?

People like the Spidells and the owner of that poor dog outside shouldn't be allowed near animals!

The second I thought of him, there he was by Pat's computer—the same African-American guy I'd biked into the day before. Grinning, dressed in a Nike running suit and a Cleveland Indians baseball cap worn backward, he didn't look much like a dog abuser.

"Mrs. Haven—Pat," I said, "that kid's messing with your computer. His dog—"

She stood on her toes to see over the cages. "Eddy?"

He glanced over, then walked toward us. "Hey! How are you?" he called to me, like he was happy to see me.

"Eddy Barker," Pat said, "I'd like you to meet Winnie Willis."

"Whinny?" He chuckled. "Like a horse makes?"

If I'd been a horse, I'd have bitten him. "Yeah. Winnie," I said. "You think that's funny? How's your dog, *Mr. Barker?*"

"Just Barker," he corrected, unruffled.

Barker? I recognized the name but couldn't remember where I'd heard it.

"You two know each other?" Pat asked.

"No," I said too quickly.

"She's Lizzy's sister," Catman explained.

Maybe I should wear a T-shirt that says "Yes—I really am Lizzy's sister."

"Your sister is the best babysitter my brothers ever had!" Barker exclaimed.

That *Barker?*

"Even Johnny loves Lizzy!" Barker went on. "And he's scared of everybody—like Macho. That's the dog you saw."

"That puppy living up to his name yet, Barker?" Pat asked. She turned to me. "Barker's trained a dog for each of his five brothers—dogs everyone else gave up on. When I found that scared li'l black-and-tan, I knew Barker was the dog's only hope."

I squirmed. "The dog was abused *before* he—?" I wanted to melt into the floor. How could I have gotten it so wrong? "I'm sorry, Barker," I said finally.

"'Bout what?" Barker's smile was so real, with nothing fake about it, that I wondered how I could have thought what I had.

"I—I thought *you* were the one who hurt the dog," I admitted.

Barker raised his eyebrows and burst into laughter that was so catching we all laughed with him. Then he checked his watch. "Whoa! I better get back to the dog e-mails."

"Dog e-mails?" I asked. "You *are* a dog genius! They even write you?"

Catman grinned with a low noise that

sounded like a purr. But Pat Haven burst into an all-out laugh that made the gerbils scamper.

"Barker set up a pet help line for locals to write in," Pat explained. "He handles the dog questions. Catman takes the cat inquiries. I try to cover everything else."

"Ring! Ring!"

I glanced at Pat, but she made no move to answer the phone.

"Ring! Ring! Ring!"

"Shouldn't somebody answer that?" I asked.

"Would you, Winnie?" Pat asked, her eyes twinkling.

I shrugged, then headed toward the ringing sound. No phone in sight, so I leaned over the counter to check behind it.

"Squawk!" Up flew the same red bird I'd seen in the barn. *"Ring! Hello! Who's there?"* he said, as he soared past me to Victoria Hawkins, the beautiful girl who looked like a Native American princess.

Victoria had just entered the store. She walked up the aisle frowning. "Peter Lory!" she called, and the bird flew to her shoulder.

"I get it," I said, pushing myself off the counter. "Like that old, scary actor, Peter Lorre. Right? Chattering lory—Peter Lorre?"

Victoria didn't crack a smile. "I need assistance. I am in rather a hurry. Where might I find high-grade cracked sunflower seeds?"

The way she asked made me feel like her personal slave. "Try a sunflower," I said and walked away.

Seeing Victoria made me picture the unfriendly Stable-Mart. The urge to be with Wild Thing tugged at me like gravity—always there whether I realized it or not. With no second job, I felt further away from buying her than ever. I wished Catman hadn't gotten my hopes up.

*N*ice to meet you," I called back at Pat as
I turned to hurry out of the pet store.

"Wait!" Barker called from the computer
corner. "Can you help with these horse questions?"

Catching a glimpse of Victoria and her bird,
I felt like breaking out of there.

"Show her the two e-mails from yesterday,"
Catman said.

"Just a minute . . ." Barker typed pretty fast.

I read the e-mail exchange he was finishing up:

> My dog hates me! I even get down on
> her level and stare into her eyes. But
> she just growls! Help!
> —Max

Barker had written:

> Max,
> Your dog doesn't hate you! She's scared!
> In dog talk, staring means, "Oh yeah!
> Wanna fight about it?" And don't get
> down on the ground with her. It scares
> her to see you change size and shape.
> Just love her. She'll love you back!
> —Barker

"Your turn," Barker said to Winnie, getting up from the wooden desk chair and motioning me to sit down.

I sat, nervous, with Pat Haven, Catman, and Barker looking on. Victoria was peering into the canary cage, but I had a feeling she was listening.

I read the e-mail:

> My pony eats so fast she chokes on her
> food! The vet says she's healthy. What
> should I do?
> —Megan

I typed:

> Megan,
> Try putting a large block of salt in the

feed trough. That should slow her
down. She'll have to keep nudging the
block out of the way to get to the
grain. And hang out with your horse at
mealtime—and all the time!
—Winnie

"Awesome!" Pat cried, resting her hand on
my shoulder.

I answered the next one about tips on buying a
good horse. Then I clicked to the last horse e-mail:

I love my horse, but he's started balk-
ing on me. I hate to bring out the whip.
Is there a cure?
—Hawk

I wrote:

Hawk,
Burn that whip! For starters, ride your
horse somewhere fun. I'll bet you ride
in circles—an arena, right? Take his
mind off balking! If you're both having
fun, he'll forget all about balking.
—Winnie

Catman turned to Pat Haven. "So?"

"Great answers if you ask me," Barker threw in.

Pat twirled one of her curls. "I can't pay much—minimum wage for the time it takes to answer. But if you'd take over the horse e-mails, Winnie, you'd do me proud."

"You mean it?" I asked, letting hope slip back in.

"I'm dog-tired of trying to come up with the answers myself!" Pat exclaimed. She glanced to the dog pen. "No offense."

It wouldn't add up to much with just a couple of e-mails a day. But it brought me that much closer to Wild Thing.

Late that night Wild Thing lifted her head as I spread my green saddle blanket in her pasture. Moonlight fingered through the trees in streaks of silvery white.

"I love you, Wild Thing," I whispered. "I wish you could believe me."

While the mare munched clover, I sang, "Mares eat oats, and does eat oats, and little lambs eat ivy." But before I knew it, I'd switched to "Amazing Grace," "How Great Thou Art," and "Jesus Loves Me."

When I got to "Jesus loves me—this I know . . . ," Wild Thing snorted.

"This I know?" I said. "This I used to know, Wild Thing. I'm just not sure. Not now."

I looked up at the stars, trying to remember what it had been like to feel God's love. "How can you love me after what I did?"

Pictures burst through my mind's blockade and flooded in—Mom and me arguing; Dad pointing to the snow swirling against the window; me pulling out the tears, knowing I could make Mom drive me to look at the new horse.

I got up so suddenly Wild Thing shied away.

Shaking my head to get rid of the pictures, I ran all the way home.

For the next five days I divided my time between Stable-Mart and Pat's Pets. Morning and night Wild Thing and I kept our secret meetings.

More horse e-mails poured in. Someone named "Hawk" sent three or four a day, asking about everything from bits and bridles to cracked hooves and riding bareback.

Hawk asked about me, too. I didn't give out my last name or where I live, even though Pat only gave the e-mail address to customers. But I did tell Hawk things I didn't usually talk about. It seemed easier "talking" about myself when I didn't have to see the other person. I wrote about Stable-Mart and my plan to earn enough money to get Wild Thing away from there.

Friday I whistled as I raked the last stall. That morning Wild Thing had let me scratch her jaw and withers for several minutes before moving off. I could still feel her softness on my fingertips.

"Hello! Peter, stop that!"

This time I recognized Peter Lory. I didn't mind the bird so much. But where Peter went, Princess Victoria couldn't be far behind.

"Have you done the stalls?" Victoria asked, leaning in to see for herself. Her red jeans and buckskin leather shirt would have looked weird on anybody else. But they made her look glamorous.

Just being around her made me feel like a Przewalski, the most primitive breed of horse. *What business is it of yours if I've done the stalls, Lady Victoria?*

Before I could say anything, a squeal pierced through to the stable. It came from the pasture.

"Wild Thing!" I cried, dropping my rake and racing outside. My heart beat like thundering hooves, shaking my whole body.

At the paddock entrance, Summer and Richard flanked Wild Thing, who reared against their long ropes as they tried to force her inside.

"Stop!" I yelled, racing toward them. "Richard, I said I'd catch her!"

Summer scooted as far away from the rearing horse as her rope allowed. "You?"

Richard wouldn't look at me. He yanked the rope, throwing Wild Thing off balance, making her hop on her hind legs.

"Leave her alone!" I screamed.

"Where do you get off?" Summer yelled back.

I moved toward the mare, my arms out to my sides, moving like a windmill. "Easy, girl."

"Get away!" Richard shouted. "You'll get hurt!"

"Hey, girl," I said, faking a calm I didn't feel. "What's with these humans, huh?"

She tossed her long, white mane in the still air. Dust stirred in clouds at her feet.

I moved in closer, stopping when I sensed her tense up.

Then Summer lost it. "Get in here, you crazy horse!" she yelled. She flicked the end of her rope, landing it on the Arabian's rump.

Wild Thing lunged forward. I dodged sideways. Then I charged at Summer. "Are you crazy?" I cried, inches from her face. "Don't you know anything about horses? She's terrified! And you hit her? What's wrong with you?"

Summer, for once, was speechless.

"Let go of that rope!" I screamed.

I wheeled on Richard, who still held his line taut. His eyes were as wide as Wild Thing's. "You too!" I shouted. "Let that horse go!"

"Winnie," he said, "go home and leave this to me. We can handle her."

But Wild Thing didn't want to be handled. She lowered her head and snorted. I sensed what was coming. She was seconds away from bucking violently.

"See?" Summer said smugly, pointing to the

horse as if Wild Thing's nose-to-the-ground position signaled defeat instead of a gathering torna-
do. "This nag just needs to know who's boss."

"She knows who's boss," I said. "And you
better get out of her way because she's about
to prove it."

Before I'd finished talking, Wild Thing burst
into the paddock like an exploding cannonball.

Summer screamed. "Help!" She let go of her
rope and fell backwards.

Richard held on. But he was no match for the
Arabian. Her galloping force jerked him off his
feet, dragging him in the dirt as the mare tore
around the paddock.

"Let go!" I shouted.

He released the rope and rolled in the dirt.
Then he jumped to his feet, swearing and cursing.
"Wait 'til I get my hands on you!" he shouted.

"No!" I cried.

The mare circled the paddock, tail high, neck
arched. The ropes dragged behind her, snakes
dancing in the dust. I wanted to unhook them,
but she wouldn't let me near her. She galloped,
stopped, changed directions, cantered, trotted—
getting as far away from us humans as she could
in that fenced-in paddock.

Richard slammed the gate so the horse couldn't get out. He stalked her, hate burning in his eyes as he muttered curses. I was terrified of what he'd do if he got hold of her.

"Summer!" he yelled. "Get over here! Now!"

Summer didn't argue. She walked back out to us.

"We'll scare her into the corner and take her down," he said.

"You can't—!" I protested.

"Shut up!" he yelled. "Summer, do as I say!" He waved his arms above his head and whooped, running at Wild Thing.

The mare pivoted, changing directions in a gallop.

"Now!" he screamed. "Summer, do it!"

They yelled, arms waving, backing Wild Thing into the corner.

The mare reared. Terror shone from her eyes as she snorted and pawed. Closer and closer they came, trapping her.

I couldn't stand it. I rushed up behind Richard and shoved him toward his sister. Wild Thing stopped rearing and stood trembling. I figured I had two seconds before she exploded. Reaching up, I unlatched her halter and yanked it off. The halter and ropes slid to the dust. "Run!" I screamed.

Wild Thing had the opening she needed to escape.

"Go, girl!" I shouted.

She took off from a standstill and raced around the paddock, gaining speed. "Jump!" I cried. "Jump!"

She raced straight for the fence and with a smooth leap, cleared it by a foot. I held my breath as she landed in the south pasture turf and kept running.

"You little—!" Richard shouted, charging at me.

Summer was right behind him. "We had her! How dare you?"

"You're both idiots!" I screamed, anger sparking behind my eyeballs. My chest heaved.

"What did you say?" Summer demanded.

"Stupid idiots!" I shouted.

"Oh yeah?" Summer yelled. "We are, are we? And do you know what you are?"

I waited. Nothing she could call me mattered. They'd wrecked everything I'd gained with Wild Thing. I'd have to start all over.

"No, you tell me, Summer," I said. "What am I?"

A smile slowly appeared on Summer Spidell's lips. "Fired!"

Fired? I looked desperately to Richard. He'd overridden Summer once. I couldn't be fired. I needed the money. I needed to be close to Wild Thing.

But Richard's expression was meaner than his sister's. "That goes double for me. Get out of here—and don't come back!"

Victoria was standing in the stable doorway,
watching everything.

"Ring! Ring! Uh-oh!" Her bird flapped its wings
and bobbed. Even *it* mocked me.

I pushed past Victoria and kept running.
I didn't stop until I found myself at Pat's Pets.

Pat Haven and Barker were settling in a new
litter of puppies. I ducked behind the fish aisle.
My vision blurred as I watched striped angelfish
swim in and out of underwater castles.

*What will happen to Wild Thing? What if the
Spidells try to break her again? I shouldn't have lost
my temper!*

"Winnie?" Barker called up. Puppies yapped.
Pat laughed. "You need something?"

I wiped my face with the back of my hand.

The horseshoe scar at my elbow whizzed under my eyes like a car out of control. "No!" I hollered back. "I—I'm going to check e-mail!"

"Good!" Pat yelled up. "Quite a few horse ones."

I moved to the computer. One kid had written:

> My buddy chased me all over the stable yelling that his Paint is better than my Pinto. What should I tell him?

I answered:

> Tell him you're both unbelievably lucky to have horses of your own. And stop running in the barn! You'll spook the horses.

I don't know how long I sat staring at the screen, trying to focus on the words in front of me. My mind felt bombarded with images of Wild Thing, pictures as real as if I were sitting in front of a television watching a horror movie— Wild Thing rearing, tugging against the ropes.

The mailbox flag symbol popped up: *You've got mail!* It was for me from Hawk. I felt as glad to hear from Hawk as if the message were coming from my best friend.

Winnie,
My horse is doing fine. I thought I'd
write to see how you're doing. How's
that Arabian?
—Hawk

Something opened inside me, and I started
typing as fast as I could. I told Hawk about
losing my temper and about losing my job.

I have to make a lot of money fast! I
have *to earn enough to buy Wild Thing!*
—Winnie

I hit Send and waited for the reply in new
mail. It didn't take long:

I've got it! The Auction! You know so
much about horses, Winnie! Go to the
auction tomorrow and buy a horse
cheap. Work with him all week. Then
next Saturday, you can sell the same
horse for a lot more money at Spidells'
fall sale!
    People assume something must be
wrong with auction horses, so they sell
cheap. But at Spidells' sale, the seller
shows off the horse, and the same

horse can sell for hundreds of dollars more. Anybody can sell there too, because Spidell takes a percentage of the sale. But you could still have enough left to buy Wild Thing—especially if they've given up on her.
—Hawk

By the time I'd finished reading, my heart was pounding and my mind racing. *It's crazy, right? Or is it? I can gentle most horses in a week. And I'd look them over carefully and get a good-natured one. But where am I going to get the money to buy a horse at auction?*

"From Dad," I muttered, getting up from the computer.

Catman and Lizzy were working on a shelter for Larry the Lizard when I ran up. In between panting breaths, I filled them in on my auction plan.

"I'll soften Dad up with my famous Missouri ham," Lizzy offered.

"Remember," Catman said, staring hard into

my eyes, "you can't *make* a cat do something he doesn't want to do."

I wasn't sure if he meant *cat,* as in the animal, or *cat,* like in old movies where hippies called each other "cat."

"Like . . . you can lead a cat to water, but you can't make him drink?" I asked.

Catman grinned. "People think I train cats. But you can't train a cat. I just get them to follow along. They think it's their own idea."

I felt like I was piecing together a Catman puzzle. "Make buying the horse Dad's idea?"

Catman didn't answer. "Good idea, Winnie. See you later." He strolled off, staring up at the sky, which had filled with heavy gray clouds and the promise of rain.

Lizzy spent the rest of the day peeling potatoes and basting a ham with chunky peanut butter. Meanwhile I cleaned the barn, which was in better condition than I'd thought. The red paint had flaked off, making it look run-down. But inside Mr. Haven had built a solid, horse-friendly barn, with large stalls that opened to pasture.

I'd finished sweeping the last stall when rain-drops plunked on the roof. The smell of hay and rain set off a slide show in my head of our Wyoming ranch.

I heard the grinding gears of our old truck.

This is it, I thought. *God, if you're still listening, please help.* I knew God had to be listening all the time. But I felt so far away, it was hard to carry on a conversation.

It was like that with Dad too, as if we'd given up on talking to each other. The first few months after the accident, Lizzy had tried every-thing to get us to talk, to make things the way they used to be. But after a while, even Lizzy could see it wasn't going to happen.

I'd have to cut through all of that—for one night at least. Wild Thing's life depended on it.

I dodged raindrops as I dashed to the house. Dad ran up the steps, his jacket over his head. I tried to open the door for him, and he tried to hold it open for me. That was the other thing that had changed since the accident—politeness. Dad and I had become too polite with each other, as if that made up for everything else that wasn't right between us.

Lizzy served dinner with candles and plates

that matched. But Dad didn't seem to notice. My stomach felt like colts were playing in it.

Dad reached for another slice of peanut-butter ham. "Found out today those bike parts I need cost a bundle."

Lizzy kicked me under the table. I tried to remember what Catman said about leading a cat to water.

"Dad," I said, forking my potatoes, "I wish I could bring in some cash around here. I mean, Lizzy's doing her part babysitting and cooking most of the meals."

"Well, it will all work out one way or the other," Dad said. "Pass the salt, please?"

I passed it. "If only I could help in some way. But all I know is horses. Of course, a lot of people make good money from horses."

Dad stared at his napkin. I knew he was thinking about Mom. Dad hadn't taken any part in the ranch. He didn't even ride.

Quickly I asked, "Have you seen the auction barn out on Baney Road?"

"I *have* seen that barn," Dad replied. "I drove by there last Saturday. Most traffic I've seen in Ashland."

"I hear lots of people make money from that

auction," Lizzy said. "Hundreds and hundreds
. . . even thousands of dollars, maybe even—"

I interrupted her before she went too far. "If
you know what you're looking for, you can get
a great bargain there. Then you'd sell the horse
somewhere else for a lot more money."

Please, God, lead my dad to water.

Dad took a sip of water and leaned back in
his chair. "Where do people sell horses around
here? The newspaper? Can't imagine there's
much of a market in the classifieds." He downed
another bite of ham and wiped the peanut
butter from his lips.

"Stable-Mart has a fall sale next Saturday," I put
in casually, trying not to look at Lizzy. Her hand
reached under the table and grabbed mine.

"So," Dad said, "say someone bought an
auction horse as an investment. What next?"

Lizzy squeezed my hand so hard, my fingers
tingled. "Then you gentle the horse and show it
off at a real sale, like Stable-Mart's," I explained.

"How long would it take to get a return on
the investment?" Dad asked, sounding like his
old business self. "You know, to tame the horse
and then resell at a profit?"

I faked a yawn. "We used to gentle our horses

in a few days. Some took longer. But most came around by the end of a week."

Dad leaned forward, elbows on the table. "Tell me everything you know about that Stable-Mart sale."

I told him everything Hawk had told me.

"Perfect!" Dad exclaimed when I'd finished. "Winnie, I've got a proposition for you!"

Thank you, Catman! . . . And thank you, God!

Dad and I worked out the details. He'd drive Lizzy and me to the auction barn early so I could look over the horses and pick a few possible "investments."

"I've only got $750 in savings, Winnie," Dad said, forking the last bite of brownie cake Lizzy had made to seal the deal. "We'll go as high as that, and no higher."

As soon as I could, I ran to my room and got the horse blanket. I couldn't wait another minute to give Wild Thing the good news.

Hang on, girl. One more week at Stable-Mart, and I'll get you out of there for good!

I'd forgotten about the change in weather. Wind brought the soft rain in at a slant as I walked to Stable-Mart. I didn't care. I still couldn't believe it. I'd led Dad to water.

But deep inside I knew there was more to it. *Okay, God. Sorry about thinking you might not be listening.*

A bright light shone from the stable as I walked around to the south pasture. The rain picked up, clattering against the metal roof and rustling the leaves.

"Wild Thing!" I called at the fence.

Rain poured down, making it impossible to see deep into the pasture. I climbed through the fence and headed out. "Here, girl!" I called.

I inhaled. I couldn't smell her.

Don't be silly. You can't smell anything in this downpour.

I listened for any sign of her—a nicker, a whinny, a snort. Anything. "Wild Thing! Where are you, girl?"

Nothing but the splash of rain answered me.

"Wild Thing?" I shouted, panic rising in me like smoke, choking me.

I ran to the end of the pasture, my tennis shoes slipping in the mud. "Wild Thing!" I screamed.

She wasn't there.

I circled in the tall, drenched grass, calling out to her.

Thunder rumbled, then boomed. Lightning struck the sky in a jagged streak that lit up the whole pasture. And I could see. Wild Thing was gone.

$\mathcal{I}$ don't know how long I sat in the pasture while rain soaked into my bones. I was too late. Wild Thing was gone.

Before I left, I checked the stable, the paddock, the other pastures. But I knew I wouldn't find the Arabian. They'd gotten rid of her. And I'd probably never know where.

Saturday morning Lizzy woke me at dawn. "Winnie!" she shouted. "We have to be at the auction in thirty minutes!"

I rolled over and faced the wall. "I'm not going."

Lizzy spent 10 minutes dragging the details out of me, and the next 10 convincing me I still had to go to the auction.

As soon as we got to the auction barn, I left Lizzy and Dad registering, while I slipped back to the holding stalls. As I examined horse after horse, I grew sadder and sadder. A sorrel American Saddle Horse could have won a beauty contest, but her cracked and bumped hooves indicated a history of poor care and lameness.

Three horses had weird teeth, altered to make them appear younger. A groove called Galvayne's groove shows up at the top of a horse's tooth at age 10 and grows longer the older the horse gets. Mom had a million stories about crooked horse dealers who'd filed off or filled the groove, stained or reshaped teeth to pass off an old horse as a young one. All three of these horses had filed teeth, but I could still feel their Galvayne's grooves.

Two others had been drugged into being quiet. I could tell by their glassy eyes.

"Is that the one to bid on?" Eddy Barker peered into the stall where I'd been checking out a black Morgan. I wondered if Barker ever frowned. So far his smile had just changed sizes.

Lizzy said the Barkers were the happiest family she'd ever seen. Catman was with Barker.

I must have looked surprised to see them. "Pat brought us," Catman explained. "Something wrong?"

"We thought you'd be psyched," Barker said. "But you look like you lost your best friend."

I *had* lost my best friend. But I didn't feel like talking about it.

"This is kind of a sad place," I admitted. "Look at this Morgan." I lifted his foreleg, where I'd spotted dozens of tiny scars.

"Pretty banged-up knees," Catman said.

"He's a stumbler," I explained, setting down his hoof. "Somebody forced him to do too much too early. He doesn't use his hocks well, so he drags his back legs." I stood back so they could see his back shoe. "Toes are worn from dragging."

"Winnie!" Dad called as he and Pat walked over to us.

"Where's Lizzy?" I asked.

Pat laughed. "Hiding! Beats me how a gal who cuddles lizards and spiders can be scared of horses!"

Dad scanned the stalls. "So where's our moneymaker?"

I showed them my three picks: a Paint mare, a bay Thoroughbred gelding, and a chestnut Arabian, who was four years older than the owner claimed and nothing like Wild Thing.

"There might be more," I said, as we joined Lizzy and the crowd in the arena. "They bring some in late."

"You hold our bidding number, Winnie," Lizzy insisted, shoving a white cardboard *34* on a popsicle stick at me. She scooted closer to Dad.

The auction began, and we watched as the first two horses went over our limit. I couldn't help comparing every horse I saw to Wild Thing. They all came up way, way short.

The Thoroughbred I'd picked trotted in.

"Is that one of ours?" Dad asked, sounding excited.

"He's so skinny . . . and ugly," Lizzy said.

"I'm counting on other people thinking the same thing." I glanced around at the crowd. "He'll clean up fine though."

Even though I still didn't want to be there—not with Wild Thing out of the picture—my stomach fluttered as the bidding started.

"Who'll give me $500 to open it up?" asked the auctioneer.

Nobody did.

"One hundred dollars!" somebody called from the crowd.

The auctioneer did his calling, trying to bid us up.

Dad elbowed me, and I lifted our number to jump in at $250 and $625. I was so nervous, I kept repeating to myself: *not over $750. $750. $750.* But we lost out to an old horseman who looked as if he'd been to a million auctions.

"You were so close!" Pat shouted. "Winnie, you sure know your horseflesh! That fella who bought that Thoroughbred was around when my husband was in the horse trade. He's as sly as a fox. No offense. "

"I liked the others better anyway," Barker said. "Didn't you, Catman?"

The next horse didn't sell. The owner had drugged the mare, but not enough. She limped in. The crowd murmured, and nobody bid.

"How much longer, Winnie?" Lizzy whined.

I started to answer her when I heard a squeal. Something in my heart felt electric. I strained to hear . . . to smell . . . to sense.

I'm going crazy. This is ridiculous. It can't be—

Through the gate came a horse that took four

men to lead. They crowded around so we couldn't get a look at the animal, who whinnied, snorted, reared, and tore at the lines holding her down.

I knew before the men moved out of the way. I knew before I saw the arch of her neck, the flare of her nostrils. *Wild Thing!*

"Man, those cats are no match for that horse," Catman said.

"They don't really think they can sell that horse, do they?" Pat asked.

"I doubt it," Dad replied. "Hope it doesn't slow things down."

"Well, they better keep it away from me!" Lizzy cried.

I couldn't speak, couldn't breathe, as I watched them jerk on the ropes. They closed her in from behind, snapping a whip to move her into the arena.

The auctioneer cleared his throat over the loudspeaker. "As you can see, you'll be bidding on a lot of horse here," he said. "Can you bring her all the way in, men?"

One of the men dropped his rope and jumped the fence as the mare lunged forward. The crowd chuckled.

. "Uh . . . what'll ya give me for this . . . spirited mare?" asked the auctioneer. "Come on, men! Don't be shy. You're not afraid of a little horse, are you?"

My stomach ached. My head throbbed. Crowd noises blurred. I could sense Wild Thing's pain as if they were pulling *me*, humiliating and terrifying *me*.

"Is he kidding?" Dad said. "Who would be crazy enough to pay for a horse like—?"

"Seven hundred and fifty dollars!" I cried, standing on my tiptoes, waving my number *34* as if I were signaling for rescue planes.

The arena fell silent. All heads turned toward me.

Lizzy gasped.

Dad made a choking sound.

The auctioneer spit into his microphone. "Sold!"

*W*innie!" Lizzy cried.

"Lizzy," I whispered, "that's Wild Thing!" I could hardly remember bidding. It was as if someone else, someone inside me, had shouted out $750. Seven hundred and fifty dollars—our limit.

Dad looked like somebody had punched him in the stomach. When he finally spoke, he sounded as if the punch had knocked the wind out of him. "Are . . . you . . . out . . . of your mind?"

"Dad, I had to—"

"That was all of our investment money!" His skin tightened around his cheeks and neck. "That was all I had. And you blew the whole thing on *that?*" He glared at Wild Thing and pointed his finger as if it were a sword.

"I can gentle her, Dad!" I insisted. "You'll see!"

"I saw!" he shouted. "We all saw! It took an army of men to get that wild creature into the arena!"

People turned to stare at us.

Dad got louder. "They should pay *us* $750 to take that horse off their hands!"

"Dad," I pleaded, "I didn't mean to bid the whole—"

Lizzy broke in. "Dad, I'm sure Winnie knows what she's doing."

Lizzy didn't look sure. But I'd never been more grateful she was my sister.

"Nobody knows more about horses than Winnie," she went on.

Dad shook his head. "That's what I used to think too."

It took me the rest of the day to lead Wild Thing home. She danced and sidestepped, trying to run ahead, forcing me to turn her in circles again and again until we were both dizzy.

Catman and Lizzy were waiting for us at home. They lifted the old gate and swung it back so I could turn Wild Thing into the pasture. When I did, she raced off as if her tail were on fire.

That night I slept in the barn on Mom's blanket as Wild Thing paced in our own pasture. It should have felt like my dream coming true. Wild Thing was actually here, just as I'd imagined her.

But it wasn't the same. She wasn't mine.

Dad hadn't spoken to me since the auction, and he had every right to be angry. There was no question of keeping Wild Thing for myself. Dad needed his investment money back. We'd have to sell the Arabian in the Stable-Mart's sale and hope somebody bid more than I had.

Still, if I could gentle her, I could make sure she ended up in a good home with people who would appreciate her. That would have to be enough.

Sunday afternoon Lizzy came to the barn as I was pulling out hay for Wild Thing. "Can't you get her to come?" Lizzy asked.

I sighed. Cupping my hands to my mouth, I hollered, "Wild Thing!"

I waited for a nicker. None came.

"Not much of a name." Catman had crept up behind us.

"How do you do that?" Lizzy asked. "Scared me half to death!"

He shielded his eyes and gazed out to the pasture. "Shouldn't you name her White Beauty or Misty or Flicka or something?"

I didn't answer, so Lizzy did. "Winnie has this thing about naming horses," she explained. "Like if she doesn't name it, she won't get attached and feel sad when it goes away."

Catman leaned down to scratch a kitten who rubbed against his ankle. "What's the plan?"

Two more cats pranced up to Catman for attention. They purred, trusting him totally.

Trust!

"My plan," I said, "is to help Wild Thing trust me, to convince her that I love her." That had been Mom's secret to gentling.

"Make her feel your love," Lizzy said softly. I risked a glance at her. Lizzy knew how hard it had been for *me* to feel love since the accident. In the beginning, she'd tell me over and over that God and Dad hadn't stopped loving me, that I just didn't feel it. I'd told her so many times to stop talking about it that she finally had.

I needed to get moving. "Don't just stand there!" I demanded. "Sing!"

Lizzy and I turned in a pretty awful version of "Amazing Grace," then two other hymns, while Catman watched.

Wild Thing paid no attention.

"Some help you are, Catman!" Lizzy scolded.

"Don't know those songs," he admitted.

"Well," Lizzy said, "you don't know what you're missing! Hymns rock! You'll have to come to church with Barker and me sometime and hear hymns on the guitar. Sounds even better than Winnie and I."

Lizzy had gone to church with the Barkers twice that I knew of. Dad and I had passed. Dad never talked much about God, not even back in Wyoming. But Mom had told us about how she and Dad had discovered Christ the same year they'd found each other: "Your dad and I met in a Christian campus meeting my second year at the University of Wyoming. I heard the most awful singing voice, turned around, and there he was."

Catman's grin brought me back to the present. Then he surprised me by bursting into song:

"Wild Thing!" he sang, tapping his foot. "You make my heart sing! You make everything—!"

Lizzy and I were laughing so hard I couldn't make out the words. But it didn't stop us from singing along as Catman plucked invisible guitar strings.

That's when I noticed Wild Thing, neck arched and ears pricked forward. "Don't look," I whispered, "but Wild Thing's jealous." Mom taught me that horses love laughter more than sugar cubes.

We forced even louder laughter until we heard a car drive up. Pat Haven and Eddy Barker hopped out. Macho, Barker's black-and-tan puppy, bounded beside him, no sign of fear.

"How's that horse?" Pat shouted.

"Coming along," I answered.

"Thought you and that wild horse might need some food," she said, tugging on the brim of her floppy hat. "Had an extra bag sitting around the store. Not my flavor." She let out one of her deep giggles. I wished Wild Thing could have heard it.

I felt so grateful I could hardly look at her. "Thanks," I muttered. "A lot."

"Nonsense!" she said, getting back in her blue car. "Well, boys!" she hollered out the window.

"Don't stand around chewing your cud—no offense to neighboring cows."

Catman and Barker hoisted a gunnysack of horse feed out of the trunk.

"I'll be praying for you *and* that horse!" Pat promised, as she jerked the car forward and drove off.

Mom would have loved Pat Haven.

Barker stayed and helped put the feed into a rubber trash can I'd already cleaned out. I scooped some oats into a metal bucket and carried it out to the pasture, shaking it to lure in the mare. But she ignored me.

Barker's dog trotted up to Lizzy, wagging his tail.

"I can't believe what you've done with this dog, Barker!" Lizzy exclaimed, scratching Macho on his belly as the dog rolled over for more. "What's your secret?"

Barker yanked something from his jeans pocket. An awful smell came with it.

"Gross!" Lizzy cried, backing away.

Macho lunged at his master as Barker peeled off the plastic wrap to unveil the grossest piece of meat I'd ever seen.

"It's barely cooked liver!" Barker said. He tore

off a piece and gave it to Macho. "You ought to see what he'll do for roadkill!" He wrapped the liver back up. "Ah . . . the way to a dog's heart is through his stomach."

"That's it!" I cried. "Lizzy, I need you to work your kitchen magic for Wild Thing. We need treats—horse treats!"

"You got it!" Lizzy said, wedging between Catman and Barker. "We've already got oatmeal and molasses in the house . . . and apples and carrots. I'll whip up a horse treat even Wild Thing can't resist!"

At dinner the kitchen smelled like molasses and oats. We ate spaghetti. Lizzy tried to get a conversation going, but Dad and I weren't much help.

After dinner Lizzy shoved a bag filled with what could have passed for granola bars at me, and I trekked out to camp under a starry sky filled with the scent of horse and molasses.

Before curling up on the blanket, I broke off pieces of treat, laying down a trail from about 50 yards out, all the way to the blanket.

"Night, Wild Thing," I said. I did my best

impersonation of a nicker, then wrapped the blanket around me and fell asleep.

I woke to a whinny that seemed part of my dream. The blanket was beaded with dew, and I shivered at the cool morning air. The only light came from the moon, but dawn was waiting behind the clouds.

"Morning, girl!" I called.

The mare tossed her head, sending her long mane waving like ocean crests. I tried to imagine a good-morning nicker from her.

"Breakfast?" I asked, remembering Lizzy's treats.

That's when I noticed that the chunk of granola bar I'd set next to the blanket was gone. I lifted the blanket and searched in the grass for the missing granola chunks, following the trail of treats. Nothing. They were all gone.

I narrowed my eyes at the Arabian, who widened her eyes at me. "You already had breakfast, didn't you, girl? Want some more?"

My heart quivered as I dug into Lizzy's bag for another bar. I held it in my open hand and walked toward Wild Thing. She nodded and pawed the ground. Her ears rotated up, back, up. Then she stretched her neck until her muzzle barely reached my hand. She lipped the treat until she had it, then crunched happily. I had her eating out of my hand!

"I love you, girl," I whispered. "Please believe me."

For an hour Wild Thing grazed, and I stroked her all over. Finally, she let me lead her to within a few feet of the barn. When I sensed her fear returning, we stopped.

"Let's play!" I said, facing her.

Mom had taught me that playing is the best way to gentle a horse. I looked around for a toy, but all I came up with was a black plastic bucket. "This will have to do," I said, rolling it out of the barn.

Wild Thing shook her head as she watched the bucket roll noisily in the dirt. I ran after it, laughing at the mare's puzzled expression.

"Your turn," I said, toeing the bucket until it rested in front of her.

She pranced up to it, sniffed and snorted. Her muzzle bumped the bucket, and it rolled. Wild Thing let out a squeal. Then she nudged it again.

"Want this?" Catman stood like a ghost in the

dancing barn dust. He held out a large rubber ball. "Cats will share."

"Perfect!" I said. "Besides, playing with a bucket could be teaching her a bad habit if she ever has to drink out of one."

If she ever . . . I wished I hadn't gone there. When I worked with Wild Thing, it was easy to forget that I was doing all of this just so we could sell her. I shoved the thought away.

Catman tossed the bright red ball at us. Wild Thing sidestepped playfully.

"Race you!" I shouted, running for the ball. She didn't race, so I got there first. "Here it comes!" I called, rolling the ball to her.

She stopped it with her nose and gave it a shove, sending the ball right to Catman's feet.

"Guess she wants you to play too," I called.

Catman joined us in an awkward game of three-way catch. Wild Thing played along, rolling the ball and making us run for it. But I sensed her caution, her distrust. We had a long way to go.

The whole Barker family came by to drive Lizzy to church for some kind of youth concert. Lizzy introduced me to the other five Barker boys: Matthew, Mark, Luke, Johnny, and

William. Mrs. Barker drove her family in a bright yellow van big enough to pass for a small school bus. Her husband sat in the very back seat between Johnny and William.

As they drove off, waving back at us, I could see why Lizzy liked the family so much. I felt bad not going with them—guilty because Mom had always seen to it that we all went to church. But that wasn't all of it. I could remember when church had felt like a part of home and loving God had come as natural as riding bareback. Now somehow the pipeline that used to run from God to my heart was all clogged up.

I wondered if that was how Wild Thing felt— blocked off from everybody, all alone where love couldn't reach her. I had to break through that. I had to make her feel my love, and I had less than a week to do it.

$\mathcal{T}$uesday a northerly breeze blew in, bringing with it a bunch of new fears for Wild Thing. She bolted when a branch cracked, shied at a candy wrapper, bucked at the breeze.

"She looks wild again," Lizzy said, safe on the other side of the fence.

Lizzy was right. The mare's wide-eyed stare was back.

I was grateful Wild Thing's fears didn't include me. But she didn't trust me enough to believe I'd keep her safe either.

I asked Lizzy to bring me the empty feed sack, which I folded into a square the size of my hand. Beginning on her neck, I rubbed her all over with the gunnysack. I felt her sway when

I got to her favorite spots—her withers, jowl, low on her neck.

When I finished, I opened the sack a fold and did it all over again, repeating the process until I was stroking her with the open bag.

"Next week, Lizzy," I said, "we'll soak the sack in water and do this again. Then if there's ever a barn fire, she'll let herself be saved with a wet blindfold."

I rested the sack on her back like a saddle blanket. "She doesn't mind pressure on her back. I'm sure she's been ridden before." I hadn't ridden since the accident, since we'd sold all our horses. Everything within me ached to ride Wild Thing. "I don't want to rush it, but by next week I bet I can ride her bareback."

Lizzy cleared her throat. "Next week, Winnie?"

I frowned over at her. "Dad hasn't said anything to you about signing up for Spidells' fall sale, has he?"

Lizzy shook her head, but looked like she wanted to say something.

"I know what you're thinking. And I'm not getting my hopes up," I said. But maybe I *was*, just a little. "I'm just saying that if he doesn't register for Saturday's sale, we have to wait for the spring sale." I took off Wild Thing's gunny-sack. She shied as a gust of wind blew a dust eddy at us. "By then, anything could happen."

Pat Haven stopped by twice a day to see how Wild Thing and I were getting along. She found two saddles and four bridles in the barn and said I was welcome to them. And in the loft we discovered a nylon lunge line good as new—30 feet long with a solid hook clasp.

The lunge line proved to be exactly what I needed. Wild Thing learned fast how to move to my voice commands. I stood in the center of an imaginary circle and held one end of the lunge line, while at the other end of the rope Wild Thing circled at a walk, a trot, or a canter, as I called out the commands.

Thursday afternoon Catman and Barker came over with Pat just as Dad's truck pulled in. "Jack!" Pat called to him. "Come see what your daughter can do with this horse!"

I hoped my nerves wouldn't travel down the lunge line to Wild Thing as my audience gathered.

But the mare ran through her paces perfectly on the lunge, circling our well-worn path.

"Well, I'll be," Dad said. "Good job, Winnie. I've gotta run, but I'd like to see you and Wild Thing work out tomorrow again."

Good job, Winnie. Before I could say anything, Dad headed back to the truck.

The truck backfired as he drove off. Wild Thing bolted, jerking my arm so hard it hurt. The line whipped through my palm with blistering heat.

"Great finish," I said as Pat and Lizzy checked my hand. "Good thing Dad didn't stick around for it." I pretended to laugh.

"Your daddy's coming back for a real show tomorrow though, sugar!" Pat said. "I'd like to see that myself. Wouldn't you, boys?"

Catman shrugged, and Barker said he wouldn't miss it. Lizzy said she'd pop popcorn.

The rest of the day Wild Thing and I took turns working and playing. By nature, Arabians like humans more than most horses do. They were bred for desert nomads who needed steady mounts and good friends. We were becoming friends. But still she held back from accepting all the love I wanted to give her.

I slept in the barn Thursday night with Catman's black-and-white kitty, Nelson, snuggled next to me. Wild Thing never came in, but she didn't wander far away.

For no reason I could figure out, Friday morning Wild Thing decided to forget everything she'd learned.

"I said *trot*, not *balk!*" I shouted from the center of our makeshift arena. "Please, girl! We have to get this right."

She stood her ground as if her hooves were glued to it.

"Okay," I said. "Don't trot. Walk on!"

She switched her tail and craned her neck to look at me. She pawed the ground and jerked against the lunge line.

I tried everything—jogging with her, starting over with commands, reversing directions. Nothing got through.

My stomach ached, and my head throbbed. Finally I walked up to her. "You may think this is fun, but I don't!"

Fun? Did I say fun?

Wild Thing wasn't the only one who had forgotten! I'd forgotten the first rule of horse gentling—have fun.

I unhooked the lunge line and let it drop. Then, dangling one of Lizzy's treats behind me, I raced out into the pasture. "Come on, girl!" I called over my shoulder.

She hesitated. Could be a trick. Then she tossed her head and galloped up behind me. She soared past, came back, circled, bucking for the fun of it. *Fun!*

I stumbled toward the pond, grabbing overhanging limbs as I slid down. "Last one in's a Spidell!" I called, tugging off my boots and wading into the cool water. Rocks at the bottom gave way to slime and mud as the water rose to my knees.

Wild Thing stood at the edge of the pond and took a long drink. Then she lifted her head and stared at me. Her reflection wavered back at her.

"You don't want to be a Spidell the rest of your life," I reasoned. "Come on in!"

Wild Thing pawed at the water. She gathered her muscles, then leaped into the pond, holding her head high like Lizzy does when she doesn't want to get her hair wet. Wild Thing swam behind me, then set her feet down and nuzzled the water, splashing both of us.

I splashed her back. And she got into it, snorting water at me, dipping her nose in. She let me hang on to her neck as she swam to the middle of the pond.

I had no idea how long we'd spent in the pond when we finally climbed out. I leaned against a fallen log and soaked up the sunshine. Wild Thing shook, splashing me again, then grazed close to my log while the warm rays dried everything except my braid.

It was the most fun I'd had in two years.

"Winnie!" Lizzy was calling from the barn.

Wild Thing and I jogged in to find our audience waiting—Lizzy, Pat, Barker, Catman . . . and Dad. I couldn't believe we'd spent the whole day playing. *Now what will I do?*

"Well, girl," I said, "I guess the show must go on—but only if it's *fun*."

"Popcorn for the show!" Lizzy announced, passing around a giant bowl that smelled heavenly.

"Far out!" Catman exclaimed.

Pat dug in for a handful of popcorn. She was wearing a cowboy hat and a smile as big as a

Wyoming sunset. "I'm so hungry, I could eat a horse!" She glanced at Wild Thing. "No offense."

"So," Barker said, his mouth full, "on with the show!"

I snapped the lunge on Wild Thing's halter. "I'm afraid I can't guarantee much. My star horse and I goofed off all day."

"Cool," Catman said, leaning on the fence.

Wild Thing worked through her gaits limber and willing.

"Not bad," Dad said, after watching us for several minutes.

But I wanted better than "not bad." I wanted to try something new, a trick Mom had taught me.

God, I feel bad asking for your help again. I forgot to thank you for the great time playing with Wild Thing in the pond. But if you're listening, would you help us out here?

I walked out to Wild Thing and scratched her chin while secretly unhooking the lunge line.

"Stay!" I said, walking back to the middle of our circle, wrapping the line like a lasso. From the center, I shouted, "Walk on!"

Wild Thing pranced around the circle as if I still held her by the line.

"Trot!" I called.

She trotted, keeping to our circle track.

"Canter!"

Wild Thing cantered in an invisible circle, legs pounding the dirt with musical rhythm. No horse could have looked more beautiful. She'd learned the *invisible trick* without any practice.

Thanks, God, I said.

When we finished, the fans went wild, and Wild Thing didn't even spook at the applause. In fact, I could tell she liked it.

Lizzy and I turned out the light and plopped into our beds exhausted. She'd spent her day combing the Ashland countryside in a big toad hunt, while I'd been playing with Wild Thing.

The moon shone through our window, and a beam of light landed on Lizzy's needlework. I couldn't read the verse from my bed, but my mind supplied the photo image:

God in his gracious kindness declares us not guilty.

I wondered if Dad ever read that verse, and if it ever made him think about forgiving me.

"Lizzy," I said, staring at the way the light

bounced off the picture frames, "has Dad said anything to you?"

"You mean about the sale tomorrow?" She yawned.

I hadn't meant about the sale. I'd pushed it out of my mind so many times, I'd almost forgotten the Stable-Mart sale *was* tomorrow.

"*Did* he say something about the sale?" I asked, my chest tightening, the thought of Spidells' fall sale refusing to be shoved down.

"Nah," Lizzy said. "I think you're right. He's been so busy with back-bike orders. I'll bet he forgot about the sale." She yawned again. "Maybe Dad will make so much money from his inventions, he won't need to sell. . . . Heavenly Father, . . ." Lizzy switched to talking to God, just like Mom used to. Her voice sounded as regular as when she talked to me or anybody else. " . . . we want to keep Wild Thing, okay? Well, Winnie does. I'm still scared to death of the creature. But anyway, you know what I mean. So—"

"Knock! Knock!" Dad said as he tapped on our open door.

"Come in, Dad!" Lizzy called.

Dad almost never came in to say good night anymore.

"Night, Dad," I said.

He came and sat on the foot of my bed. "Winnie, I've got to hand it to you." He wiggled my foot the way he used to do when I was really little. "I never thought you could pull it off—I admit that. *And* I apologize for getting so upset last Saturday. But you've done it. I think we'll make a lot of money on that horse after all."

I couldn't speak.

Lizzy could. "And by the time we're ready to put her up for sale, Winnie will be able to ride her. I'll bet—"

"No time for that," Dad said.

I couldn't breathe.

Lizzy bolted up in bed. "What do you mean, no time? Why won't she have time?"

Dad laughed. "Lizzy, didn't you know that sale's tomorrow? We're all registered to go early too. Should be buyers from all over the state."

Darkness swept over the room as the moon hid behind clouds. The verses disappeared.

Dad stood up. "Get some sleep, girls. Tomorrow we get our investment back on that horse."

$\mathcal{S}$aturday morning Catman and Lizzy came out to the barn to see me off. I'd told Dad I'd lead Wild Thing to the sale in case she gave us trouble loading. I didn't think she'd act up, but I needed time. I had a plan—a plan I hadn't told anybody about, not even Lizzy. Especially not Lizzy. She'd never understand.

"Wanna hug?" Catman asked.

Surprised, I looked up to see him holding out Nelson. Embarrassed, I pet the kitty.

"It will all be okay," Lizzy said in that cheery voice of hers.

Right. All okay.

"I know how you feel," Lizzy went on. "I understand—"

"*You* understand?" Lizzy didn't even like

horses. She had her stupid bugs and lizards. Nobody was selling *them.* "You have no idea how I feel, Lizzy!"

Anger started in my chest and bubbled up with a force that frightened me. *"Mom* would have understood!"

Lizzy's eyes pooled with tears. "I miss Mom too," she said quietly.

"It's not the same!" I shouted. Wild Thing sidestepped nervously. "She was the only one who understood me! Everybody understands you, Lizzy!"

The kitten mewed and hopped out of Catman's hands.

Lizzy didn't flinch. "Maybe you're right. Maybe I don't understand you, Winnie."

I turned to Wild Thing. "Big surprise," I muttered.

"But God *does* understand, Winnie," Lizzy said.

That did it. I dropped the leadrope and wheeled on my sister. "No! He doesn't understand either!"

Catman stared at his canvas shoes.

Lizzy's voice was a whisper. "Jesus lived inside skin like ours so he'd understand. He knows, Winnie. And he loves you. You have to believe God loves you."

"Not anymore!" I shouted. My hand went automatically to the horseshoe scar above my elbow. I fought back the photos that pushed their way into my brain—the car turning over and over, Mom not moving.

"Nobody blames you, Winnie," Lizzy said.

"You don't know!" I shouted, grabbing the leadrope and pulling Wild Thing after me. "Just leave me alone!"

Wild Thing was the sweetest she'd ever been as we walked to Stable-Mart, taking the shortcut through pastures. She nuzzled me from behind whenever I got a step ahead.

"Don't be so nice, girl," I said. That was my plan. I had to show them the worst possible side of her. Spidells wanted to believe the horse was wild. If everybody believed it, then nobody would buy her.

I couldn't think beyond that. All I knew was that I couldn't let her go.

Taking the Stable-Mart driveway, we passed a dozen cars, some of them out-of-state. Richard drove by and rolled down the window of his red sports car. *"That's* Wild Thing?" he asked.

The mare was following me in a flat-footed walk, not shying at cars.

"Yeah," I said. "She refused to load. I'm afraid she's still horribly wild."

He drove off, not looking convinced.

I shook Wild Thing's leadrope, trying to get her excited, but she thought I was playing. She tossed her head. I faked jumping out of the way, in case anyone was watching. We moved to the far side of the stable while buyers filtered through the barn to the arena.

Victoria Hawkins appeared out of nowhere. "How's your horse?"

"Awful! Just terrible!" I exclaimed.

"She looks good," Victoria said.

"So I'm lying?" I shouted at her.

She held up her palm. "Easy. Sor-ry."

Dad drove up in our truck, with Lizzy and Catman in the cab. Pat Haven and Barker followed them in Pat's blue Neon. I ducked behind the stable, where I could listen to the action without seeing it.

Spidells ran the sale like the Kentucky Derby, with fanfare and loudspeakers. Wild Thing didn't even jump when the speakers came on.

The first two horses up for sale were shown off by Summer Spidell. I heard the catalog details—show horses, in their prime, champion sires, winning records. But the bidding didn't come over the loudspeakers.

I didn't have a clue how much the horses had gone for until Dad came running up to me. "Winnie, I can't believe those horses sold for $4,500 and $7,750! Of course, we can't expect a price like those. But with so many bidders out there, who knows?"

"Wild Thing's pretty wild today," I said, wishing she would do something besides graze peacefully.

Dad reached over and petted her for the first time. "Winnie, you've done an amazing job on this horse. You should feel good about it no matter what we get."

I didn't feel good about anything as Dad left. I felt awful for Wild Thing and awful for Dad. My head buzzed, and I couldn't think straight. But I kept coming back to the one thing I did know—I couldn't let Wild Thing go.

"Next up—Willis's Arabian!" Mr. Spidell's voice over the loudspeakers startled me. But the mare stayed calm.

I jiggled Wild Thing's leadrope and clapped my hands. "Come on!" I whispered. "Act up!"

Wild Thing stared at me.

"I'm not playing!" I shouted. Her eyes widened as I jerked her into the arena.

Two men stood at the gate, one with a clipboard. "Nice conformation," he said. "She'd bring a good resell price in Pennsylvania."

I pretended to have trouble with her as I led her around the arena in front of 50 or 60 onlookers.

The loudspeaker praised the white Arabian: " . . . led by a child! Good ground manners. Only five years old."

My ears were ringing. Wild Thing's steady *clip-clop* pounded like my heart.

We reached the far side of the arena, away from the crowd.

"Wild Thing," I whispered, my words choking in my throat, "please believe that I love you."

I took a deep breath and flicked the end of the rope at her, behind my back where no one could see.

She jerked, but she stayed with me, forgave me for it.

"Go!" I cried.

She wouldn't leave me.

My stomach ached at the sight of her wide eyes, white with suspicion. I swallowed, then snapped her with the rope. It couldn't have hurt her, but it scared her. She'd trusted me.

I lifted my arms suddenly. "Get out of here!"

Frightened, she reared, then bolted toward the fence. I jumped to the side, crashing into the dirt, rolling over in time to see her sail over the fence and run terrified into the pasture.

Dad and Lizzy were at my side as I got up.

"Winnie, are you okay?" Lizzy asked, reaching for me.

"That crazy horse!" Dad cried. "Winnie, are you hurt?"

I stumbled to my feet, tears stinging my cheeks.

"That stupid, no-good horse!" Dad said. "I never should have—!"

"No!" I cried. I couldn't stand it. "She's not stupid! She's wonderful! And kind. And honest."

"Winnie," Dad said, "I know you wanted this to work out. But that horse—"

Everything was wrong. "Oh, Dad," I said, sobbing and shaking. "I'm sorry! I'm so sorry!"

"What?" Dad looked pained, confused. "It's not your fault."

"It *is* my fault! Everything's my fault! I made her act up like that! I didn't want anybody to buy her. But I messed it up like I messed everything up."

At the corners of my vision, a blur of people swam together—Catman and Barker and Pat.

"I'm so sorry, Dad!" I said. "Sorry for *everything!*"

"What are you saying, Winnie?" Dad asked. He looked as frightened as Wild Thing had.

"I'm sorry I killed Mom." I said it softly, and nobody spoke. Nobody moved.

Dad's face turned white. As I stared at him, the pictures pushed at my brain: Dad saying, "Don't go, honey. It's too icy"; Mom and I getting into the car; Dad coming into my hospital room and telling me Mom had died in the wreck.

"It was all my fault," I said, feeling like I might vomit. "If Mom hadn't driven me to see that horse, she'd still be alive."

Dad got down on one knee and held me by my shoulders. "Listen to me, Winnie. The accident wasn't your fault. I *never* thought it was your fault—not for a minute! Honey, I am so sorry."

"*You?* You don't have anything to be sorry about! You didn't want her to take me to see that horse. You told her it was too icy!"

"No, honey. You know your mother. Nothing either one of us said made a bit of difference! She'd made up her mind. That's how she was—about horses, about you. It . . . was . . . an . . . accident," Dad said slowly, not letting go of my shoulders. "I had no idea you felt it was your fault. I've been so caught up just trying to get myself from one day to the next. . . . But I should have seen it, Winnie. I love you."

I jerked away. "You *can't!* Not after what I did! You can't love me!"

I broke free from Dad's grip and ran, shoving past Barker and Catman, through the crowd and out the arena. I heard Lizzy holler after me. Other voices yelled. But I kept running until I couldn't hear them.

Wild Thing stood on the crest of the hill, her neck arched, the old fear and wildness back to protect her. Protect her from me.

"I'm sorry!" I yelled. My knees buckled, and I crumpled to the ground. She'd never forgive me. Why should she? Why should anybody?

I covered my head and cried until no more tears came. "I love you, Wild Thing," I muttered. "You have to believe I love you."

Lizzy's voice replayed in her mind: *"God understands. You have to believe God loves you."*

151

Was Lizzy right? Could God possibly understand what I was feeling? I understood Wild Thing's pain, felt it almost as clearly as I felt my own.

Do you feel my pain like that, God? Do you still love me? Can you ever forgive me?

I felt a hot breath at the back of my neck.

"Wild Thing!"

Her breath, heating the hairs on my neck, made me shiver.

I got up. She let me fling my arms around her and press my cheek against her neck. "Can *you* forgive me?" I whispered. I inhaled her warm, horse smell. "It's okay. It's all okay."

The crooked thread letters of Lizzy's needlework flashed into my brain again: *God in his gracious kindness declares us not guilty. Jesus didn't die for nothing!*

God's gracious kindness. I didn't have to feel guilty, not for anything! *Jesus didn't die for nothing!*

Thank you, I prayed, as something inside of me unclogged, opening passages to my heart.

The leadrope still hung from her halter. I threaded the lead through her halter to form makeshift reins. Then I stroked her back until her muscles relaxed.

Standing at her shoulder, I swung myself up on her back. She pranced, surprised, but pleased.

I leaned forward and hugged her neck. "Let's ride," I whispered, my thighs pressing in slightly.

She read my mind and took off at a canter. We raced through the pasture, the wind blowing, the sun shining. Riding again was like a piece of me being grafted back into my body. I wished Mom could have been here to ride with me. But I could think about her now without the guilt.

And right behind the forgiveness and grace, love was waiting. It flooded over me like a Wyoming river, flowing deep inside where nothing else had reached for so long.

Mom's needlepoint verse appeared in my head as clearly as if I were watching her stitch the letters:

> For your unfailing love is as high as
>   the heavens.
> Your faithfulness reaches to the clouds.
>
> —PSALM 57:10

I felt it—that unfailing love. And I knew Wild Thing felt it too. It surrounded us like fog, like the fog on that day when I'd first run into her.

153

I could have ridden like that forever. But I knew now that whatever happened, God was watching. And he loved us. *Please,* I prayed, *give her a great home.*

"Let's go back and show them you don't deserve a name like Wild Thing," I said.

Laying the rope across her neck, I reined her back toward the arena. We got to the gate at the same moment a sale horse was being led out. Wild Thing cantered straight in, slowing to a rocking, gentle gait.

Richard spotted us first. "Look out! It's the Arabian!" he shouted.

Wild Thing and I moved as one around the arena. She wanted to please me, and she did, responding to every cue. When we pulled to a stop in front of the crowd, they burst into applause.

Spider Spidell's astonished voice came over the speakers. "Ladies and gentlemen! I believe we have another horse to bid on."

I fought back the tears. I'd done what I could to get Wild Thing a good home. The rest would be up to God.

"So," Mr. Spidell shouted out, "who'll start the bidding?"

Summer Spidell rushed past me to get to her dad. "Daddy! I want that horse! I have to have her! She could win State Champion!"

"She's a good-looker, all right," her father admitted.

"Do whatever you have to, Daddy!" Summer wheeled and pointed a red fingernail at us. "I want that horse!"

Please, God, don't let Summer get Wild Thing!

Victoria shoved her way up to Summer. *Lord, I prayed, I'd rather see Victoria Hawkins get this horse than have her go to Summer!*

Mr. Spidell cleared his throat into the microphone. "Then I guess I'll start the bidding at—"

"Wait a minute!" Dad pushed his way through the crowd. "We have a problem." He walked over and stroked Wild Thing's head.

"A problem?" Mr. Spidell asked.

"There's been a mistake," Dad said, straightening the mare's forelock. "This one's not for sale."

"No fair!" shouted Summer Spidell, her voice caught over the loudspeakers.

I leaned forward, wondering if I'd heard wrong. "Dad?"

"Come on now, Mr. Willis," Mr. Spidell said. "This horse might just bring a very good price today. Are you telling me you can't use the money?"

Dad sighed. "This horse already has an owner." He winked at me.

I stared at him. *Already has an owner?* I hugged Wild Thing's neck, then looked up. "But we can't afford—"

"We'll make it," Dad said. "Your mother always said God's love could see us through anything. All things are possible with God, right?"

I looked from Dad to Lizzy, who was crying next to him. God's love—they felt it too.

I swung my leg over and slid off my horse. "Thanks, Dad," I said, hugging him, being hugged. Lizzy wriggled in for a three-way hug. "Thanks, Lizzy," I whispered. "You were right."

Dad called over to Mr. Spidell. "Listen! If you need a horse gentled though, call my daughter— Winnie the Horse Gentler."

Lizzy glanced around at the onlookers. "Did all of you hear that?" she shouted. "Winnie the Horse Gentler is in town!"

It was a great idea. I could gentle horses for other people! I'd make enough money to keep us in feed and help out at home.

"And I shall be moving Towaco to Winnie's barn as soon as she will allow," Victoria said.

"Victoria!" Summer shouted.

"Do not call me Victoria," she said, her head held princess-high.

"Isn't that your name?" Lizzy asked.

Victoria Hawkins shook her head. "Call me Hawk."

"Hawk?" I repeated. "No way!" I stared at her. She couldn't be Hawk, not *my* Hawk.

The slightest grin passed across Victoria's lips as she asked me, "Read any good e-mails lately?"

"You!" I couldn't have been more surprised if I'd discovered I'd been writing to a real hawk. "That was *you* writing to the pet help line?" I asked, walking over to her. Hawkins—Hawk. Not even once did I make that connection.

"But why didn't you—?" I stopped. I knew why she hadn't told me she was Hawk. Hawk and I were friends. Victoria and I were not.

"Thanks, Hawk," I said, shaking her hand. "I'd love to work with Towaco."

Barker came up and shook Hawk's hand too. "Hawk," he said. "I like it."

Pat Haven had cried so hard her mascara

dripped off her face in black, watery streaks. "I'm proud as a peacock of all of you," she said, giving Hawk a huge hug. "No offense."

Mr. Spidell had apparently gotten fed up with us. Over the loudspeakers he said, "Could we get on with our sale, please?"

Richard Spidell rushed up. "Winnie, get Wild Thing out of here!"

"Don't call her that!" I snapped. "She's not wild, and she's not a thing!"

"Good," Catman said, pulling Nelson from his pocket. He walked up to the Arabian and put the cat on her back. The kitty purred, and the horse craned her neck around to see, then seemed to approve. "So what will you name her?"

I hadn't dared think of a name. I glanced over at the beautiful white Arabian. "A name," I muttered, trying to think of one that would be good enough. "Any ideas, girl?"

Her ears flicked back, then up. A scratching noise started in her chest, moved through her neck, and came out a low nicker.

"Did you hear that?" I cried.

Catman stood the closest to me. I threw my arms around him and hugged him. "She nickered!"

I ran to her and pressed my cheek against her jaw.

She nickered again. It was the warmest, friendliest greeting in the whole world.

"That's it!" I said, stepping back to look into her deep, brown eyes. "You've just named yourself. Nickers! From now on, we're Winnie and Nickers!"

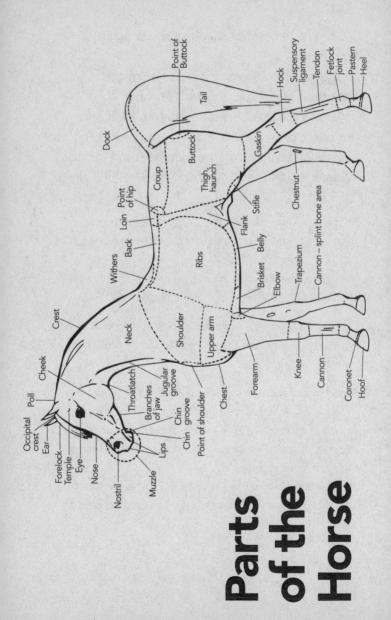

Parts
of the
Horse

🐎 Horse Talk!

Horses communicate with one another . . . and with us, if we learn to read their cues. Here are some of the main ways a horse talks:

Whinny—A loud, long horse call that can be heard from a half mile away. Horses often whinny back and forth.
Possible translations: Is that you over there? Hello! I'm over here! See me? I heard you! What's going on?

Neigh—To most horse people, a neigh is the same as a whinny. Some people call any vocalization from a horse a neigh.

Nicker—The friendliest horse greeting in the world. A nicker is a low sound made in the throat, sometimes rumbling. Horses use it as a warm greeting for another horse or a trusted person. A horse owner might hear a nicker at feeding time.
Possible translations: Welcome back! Good to see you. I missed you. Hey there! Come on over. Got anything good to eat?

Snort—This sounds like your snort, only much louder and more fluttering. It's a hard exhale, with the air being forced out through the nostrils.
Possible translations: Look out! Something's wrong out there! Yikes! What's that?

Blow—Usually one huge exhale, like a snort, but in a large burst of wind.
Possible translations: What's going on? Things aren't so bad. Such is life.

Squeal—This high-pitched cry that sounds a bit like a scream can be heard a hundred yards away.
Possible translations: Don't you dare! Stop it! I'm warning you! I've had it—I mean it! That hurts!

Grunts, groans, sighs, sniffs—Horses make a variety of sounds. Some grunts and groans mean nothing more than boredom. Others are natural outgrowths of exercise.

*****

Horses also communicate without making a sound. You'll need to observe each horse and tune into the individual translations, but here are some possible versions of nonverbal horse talk:

EARS

Flat back ears—When a horse pins back its ears, pay attention and beware! If the ears go back slightly, the horse may just be irritated. The closer the ears are pressed back to the skull, the angrier the horse.

Possible translations: I don't like that buzzing fly. You're making me mad! I'm warning you! You try that, and I'll make you wish you hadn't!

Pricked forward, stiff ears—Ears stiffly forward usually mean a horse is on the alert. Something ahead has captured its attention.

Possible translations: What's that? Did you hear that? I want to know what that is! Forward ears may also say, I'm cool and proud of it!

Relaxed, loosely forward ears—When a horse is content, listening to sounds all around, ears relax, tilting loosely forward.

Possible translations: It's a fine day, not too bad at all. Nothin' new out here.

Uneven ears—When a horse swivels one ear up and one ear back, it's just paying attention to the surroundings.

Possible translations: Sigh. So, anything interesting going on yet?

Stiff, twitching ears—If a horse twitches stiff ears, flicking them fast (in combination with overall body tension), be on guard! This horse may be terrified and ready to bolt.

Possible translations: Yikes! I'm outta here! Run for the hills!

Airplane ears—Ears lopped to the sides usually means the horse is bored or tired.
Possible translations: Nothing ever happens around here. So, what's next already? Bor-ing.

Droopy ears—When a horse's ears sag and droop to the sides, it may just be sleepy, or it might be in pain.
Possible translations: Yawn . . . I am so sleepy. I could sure use some shut-eye. I don't feel so good. It really hurts.

TAIL

Tail switches hard and fast—An intensely angry horse will switch its tail hard enough to hurt anyone foolhardy enough to stand within striking distance. The tail flies side to side and maybe up and down as well.
Possible translations: I've had it, I tell you! Enough is enough! Stand back and get out of my way!

Tail held high—A horse who holds its tail high may be proud to be a horse!
Possible translations: Get a load of me! Hey! Look how gorgeous I am! I'm so amazing that I just may hightail it out of here!

Clamped-down tail—Fear can make a horse clamp its tail to its rump.
Possible translations: I don't like this; it's scary. What are they going to do to me? Can't somebody help me?

164

Pointed tail swat—One sharp, well-aimed swat of the tail could mean something hurts there.
Possible translations: Ouch! That hurts! Got that pesky fly.

OTHER SIGNALS

Pay attention to other body language. Stamping a hoof may mean impatience or eagerness to get going. A rear hoof raised slightly off the ground might be a sign of irritation. The same hoof raised, but relaxed, may signal sleepiness. When a horse is angry, the muscles tense, back stiffens, and the eyes flash, showing extra white of the eyeballs. One anxious horse may balk, standing stone still and stiff legged. Another horse just as anxious may dance sideways or paw the ground. A horse in pain might swing its head backward toward the pain, toss its head, shiver, or try to rub or nibble the sore spot. Sick horses tend to lower their heads and look dull, listless, and unresponsive.

As you attempt to communicate with your horse and understand what he or she is saying, remember that different horses may use the same sound or signal, but mean different things. One horse may flatten her ears in anger, while another horse lays back his ears to listen to a rider. Each horse has his or her own language, and it's up to you to understand.

Horse-O-Pedia

American Saddlebred (or American Saddle Horse)—A showy breed of horse with five gaits (walk, trot, canter, and two extras). They are usually high-spirited, often high-strung; mainly seen in horse shows.

Appaloosa—Horse with mottled skin and a pattern of spots, such as a solid white or brown with oblong, dark spots behind the withers. They're usually good all-around horses.

Arabian—Believed to be the oldest breed or one of the oldest. Arabians are thought by many to be the most beautiful of all horses. They are characterized by a small head, large eyes, refined build, silky mane and tail, and often high spirits.

Bay—A horse with a mahogany or deep brown to reddish-brown color and a black mane and tail.

Blind-age—Without revealing age.

Buck—To thrust out the back legs, kicking off the ground.

Buckskin—Tan or grayish-yellow-colored horse with black mane and tail.

Cattle-pony stop—Sudden, sliding stop with drastically bent haunches and rear legs; the type of stop a cutting, or cowboy, horse might make to round up cattle.

Chestnut—A horse with a coat colored golden yellow to dark brown, sometimes the color of bays, but with same-color mane and tail.

D ring—The D-shaped, metal ring on the side of a horse's halter.

English Riding—The style of riding English or Eastern or Saddle Seat, on a flat saddle that's lighter and leaner than a Western saddle. English riding is seen in three-gaited and five-gaited Saddle Horse classes in horse shows. In competition, the rider posts at the trot and wears a formal riding habit.

Gait—Set manner in which a horse moves. Horses have four natural gaits: the walk, the trot or jog, the canter or lope, and the gallop. Other gaits have been learned or are characteristic to certain breeds: pace, amble, slow gait, rack, running walk, etc.

Gelding—An altered male horse.

Hackamore—A bridle with no bit, often used for training Western horses.

Halter—Basic device of straps or rope fitting around a horse's head and behind the ears. Halters are used to lead or tie up a horse.

Leadrope—A rope with a hook on one end to attach to a horse's halter for leading or tying the horse.

Lipizzaner—Strong, stately horse used in the famous Spanish Riding School of Vienna. Lipizzaners are born black and turn gray or white.

Lunge line (longe line)—A very long lead line or rope, used for exercising a horse from the ground. A hook at one end of the line is attached to the horse's halter, and the horse is encouraged to move in a circle around the handler.

Mare—Female horse.

Morgan—A compact, solidly built breed of horse with muscular shoulders. Morgans are usually reliable, trustworthy horses.

Mustang—Originally, a small, hardy Spanish horse turned loose in the wilds. Mustangs still run wild in protected parts of the U.S. They are suspicious of humans, tough, hard to train, but quick and able horses.

Paddock—Fenced area near a stable or barn; smaller than a pasture. It's often used for training and working horses.

Paint—A spotted horse with Quarter Horse or Thoroughbred bloodlines. The American Paint Horse Association registers only those horses with Paint, Quarter Horse, or Thoroughbred registration papers.

Palomino—Cream-colored or golden horse with a silver or white mane and tail.

Palouse—Native American people who inhabited the Washington–Oregon area. They were hightly skilled in horse training and are credited with developing the Appaloosas.

Pinto—Spotted horse, brown and white or black and white. Refers only to color. The Pinto Horse Association registers any spotted horse or pony.

Przewalski—Perhaps the oldest breed of primitive horse. Also known as the Mongolian Wild Horse, the Przewalski Horse looks primitive, with a large head and a short, broad body.

Quarter Horse—A muscular "cowboy" horse reminiscent of the Old West. The Quarter Horse got its name from the fact that it can outrun other horses over the quarter mile. Quarter Horses are usually easygoing and good-natured.

Rear—To suddenly lift both front legs into the air and stand only on the back legs.

Roan—The color of a horse when white hairs mix with the basic coat of black, brown, chestnut, or gray.

Sorrel—Used to describe a horse that's reddish (usually reddish-brown) in color.

Stallion—An unaltered male horse.

Standardbred—A breed of horse heavier than the Thoroughbred, but similar in type. Standardbreds have a calm temperament and are used in harness racing.

Tack—Horse equipment (saddles, bridles, halters, etc.).

Thoroughbred—The fastest breed of horse in the world, they are used as racing horses. Thoroughbreds are often high-strung.

Tie short—Tying the rope with little or no slack to prevent movement from the horse.

Trakehner—Strong, dependable, agile horse that can do it all—show, dressage, jump, harness.

Western Riding—The style of riding as cowboys of the Old West rode, as ranchers have ridden, with a traditional Western saddle, heavy, deep-seated, with a raised saddle horn. Trail riding and pleasure riding are generally Western; more relaxed than English riding.

Wind sucking—The bad, and often dangerous, habit of some stabled horses to chew on fence or stall wood and suck in air.

🐎 Author Talk

Dandi Daley Mackall grew up riding horses, taking her first solo bareback ride when she was three. Her best friends were Sugar, a Pinto; Misty, probably a Morgan; and Towaco, an Appaloosa; along with Ash Bill, a Quarter Horse; Rocket, a buckskin; Angel, the colt; Butch, anybody's guess; Lancer and Cindy, American Saddlebreds; and Moby, a white Quarter Horse. Dandi and husband, Joe; daughters, Jen and Katy; and son, Dan (when forced) enjoy riding Cheyenne, their Paint. Dandi has written books for all ages, including Little Blessings books, Degrees of Guilt: *Kyra's Story*, Degrees of Betrayal: *Sierra's Story*, *Love Rules*, and *Maggie's Story*. Her books (about 400 titles) have sold more than 4 million copies. She writes and rides from rural Ohio.

Visit Dandi at www.dandibooks.com

S·T·A·R·L·I·G·H·T

Animal Rescue

More than just animals need rescuing in this new series. Starlight Animal Rescue is where problem horses are trained and loved, where abandoned dogs become heroes, where stray cats become loyal companions. And where people with nowhere to fit in find a place to belong.

Entire series available now!

#1   Runaway

#2   Mad Dog

#3   Wild Cat

#4   Dark Horse

Read all four to discover how a group of teens cope with life and disappointment.

WWW.TYNDALE.COM/KIDS

CP0264

COLLECT ALL EIGHT BOOKS!

CP0015-B

Can't get enough of Winnie? Visit her Web site to read more about Winnie and her friends plus all about their horses.

IT'S ALL ON WINNIETHEHORSEGENTLER.COM

There are so many fun and cool things to do on Winnie's Web site; here are just a few:

★ PAT'S PETS
Post your favorite photo of your pet and tell us a fun story about them

★ ASK WINNIE
Here's your chance to ask Winnie questions about your horse

★ MANE ATTRACTION
Meet Dandi and her horse, Chestnut!

★ THE BARNYARD
Here's your chance to share your thoughts with others

★ AND MUCH MORE!

CP0016

The Wormling

From the minds of Jerry B. Jenkins and Chris Fabry comes a thrilling new action-packed fantasy that pits ultimate evil against ultimate good.

Book I
The Book of the King

Book II
The Sword of the Wormling

Book III
The Changeling

Book IV
The Minions of Time

Book V
The Author's Blood

All 5 books available now!

CP0138